THE GAY DETECTIVE

Simon Leaton

DEDICATION

To my Keith,
Mum. Dad, Steve, Trev, Rick
and a very special
Thank you

To Joy x

CONTENTS

ACKNOWLEDGMENTS

Wimborne, Poole and Dorset in general, the true inspiration has to be
acknowledged
and
Keith my no1 fan and critic.

1 PUSSY IN THE WELL

'Ding dong bell, pussy's in the well. That friggin nursery rhyme sends bloody chills down my spine every time I hear it.' Arthur Jay stated.

Arthur was an aging 65 year old. He smoked, drank and had a succession of on off relationships with women. Rumour had it that he had several children and Grandchildren around, not that they bothered to see him and, to be honest, he wouldn't be able to put a name to any of them either so chances are he'd probably pass them in the street without raising an eye, or that is how people perceived and gossiped about him. The truth may have been somewhat different.

Matt Powers sat opposite him in the untidy little office, patiently listening to the old man once again regale the tale of a stuck pussy down an old well, a cat belonging to the ancient Miss Allmes who had called upon Arthur's services to search for Bepe. Unfortunately, Arthur found the feline Ninja. The well was situated at the bottom of Miss Allmes cottage garden and Arthur had found a piece of rope, tied one end to an old tree stump and carefully slid down the well which was cavernous and dried up. Unfortunately the rope snapped, the cat miraculously shot up the wall like Spiderman and flew into the arms of the grumpy and humourless Miss Allmes, who then scolded the cat and walked back into the cottage, completely ignoring the cries of Arthur who sat on his backside at the bottom of a well with only a bruised ego and no way of escape.

Matt let him continue nodding here and there; he was Arthur's understudy and junior private investigator at The Wimborne Happiness Detective Agency. Well, as junior as a 38 year old ex-unemployed ex-Teacher can get. He'd been with Arthur for five months and was already on the umpteenth rendition of the pussy in the well case. Matt, it could be said, was a trier. He tried and invariably failed at all his jobs and even tried and failed at an eight year marriage, more to the fact that his wife Isabelle had been having a nine year affair with the vicar that married them in a nearby town. Matt walked around with the world on his shoulders, a broken man, but one day, not long after he had found that his teaching skills were no longer required and coming home to find Vicar Dennis was bouncing up and down with Isabelle on his marital bed, he came across an advert in a local shop window JUNIOR INVESTIGATOR REQUIRED FOR BUSY DORSET DETECTIVE AGENCY - GOOD RATES OF PAY. Matt looked at his reflection in the window, he was average height, his medium length straight fair hair and blue eyes suddenly transformed into a slick American styled PI, Yes Matt Powers P.I. had a certain ring to it. But just then his own imagination turned against him as the handsome reflection turned into something resembling Columbo with dirty hair and a scruffy rain coat. So much for self-esteem, Matt thought, so set off and applied anyway, what did he have to lose?

On entering Arthur's office for the first time, all romantic notions of being a private investigator were quashed. The office sat above Bunty's Butchers on the square of the quaint little English market town of Wimborne. He had been living and indeed grew up in the port of Poole a few miles south, until that fateful day and his wife's indiscretion, the image of the vicars' buttocks undulating above his wife's spread legs made it synonymous with pain and failure. The office was a mess, two sash windows let light stream into a small square room, two desks and reams of paper scattered everywhere, along with half consumed bottles of whisky. It stank, not so much of whisky, which in itself was surprising but of a damp airless room that never had its windows opened.

Five months later Matt had proven himself as a cleaner at the very least. The paperwork was at last sorted into folders, although still scattered about the room, windows were often opened airing the room nicely but the whisky bottles were now hidden in the bottom draw of a new filing cabinet.

The phone rang just as Arthur was on the part of the story where the fire brigade had been alerted by Miss Allmes' neighbour after hearing what she took as a fox stuck down the well. Arthur was finally free, Miss Allmes refused to take his call and driving off in a huff he had accidently run the little cat over, The cat that had caused so much trouble. Bepe was dead without a hope of recovery, flat with an air of contempt spread across his face. The witnesses were plenty but the police eventually dropped the case of cat slaughter when Miss Allmes' sister came to live with her bringing Snuggles the toy poodle.

Arthur almost dived into the pile of files and eventually surfaced with phone receiver in hand 'Hello? Who's that, speak damn it, you're paying for the call so say something. Oh hello Miss Allmes, you won't believe this but I was just singing your praises to my colleague, what? Noises down your well again, forgive me but don't you think you had better call the fire brigade? Oh I see well I would but cash flow is a little tight at the moment…'

'You're telling me!' Matt added, he was living well below the poverty line, whatever that was. At present he lived in his Volkswagen camper van behind the butchers. If he was lucky Bunty would give him some meat off cuts on certain days.

'Shhh!' Arthur sounded, briefly putting his hand over the receiver.

Matt began to tidy the files into piles against the wall.

'Money upfront? Oh, I see. Well, my assistant could certainly come take a look.'

Matt shook his head vehemently. 'No way!'

Arthur waved his hand down while trying to listen. 'You only trust me? Oh right. Well, if it's cash up front too how can I refuse? I'll just check my diary; you want me over there now? Well yes, tricky, if you'd like to hold a moment.' Arthur placed his hand over the phone receiver and reached into the drawer with his other, he produced a glass of what appeared to be pure whisky which he swigged down in one, belched then returned to the conversation. 'Yes that'll be fine Miss Allmes. I've just rearranged some business that my assistant can attend to so I'll be right over. Um, just one thing, it is cash not cheque up front? That's lovely, see you anon.'

'Assistant!! I have slaved to get this place ship shape. Since I've been here I have sorted two divorces, a lost cat and a fake telephone repair man robbing old people, what have you done?'

'Relax my boy, I coordinate don't I?' Arthur sits back, producing his trusted glass of whisky again.

Matt almost bursts 'Coordinate, coordinate! Count all the money I make the business, incidentally when am I getting paid? It's been seven weeks without me seeing a bean.'

'I give you money to buy food. Anyway, as I keep telling you, one day all this will be yours, you can do what you like with it then.' Arthur smiled a crooked half pickled expression.

'Oh there is just no reasoning with you is there? Do you want a lift to Miss Allmes?'

'No, no I'll drive myself thank you.'

'You can't, you old soak. You must be over the limit.'

'I'm taking the push bike! You don't half get your knickers in a twist boy.'

'You're still over the limit.'

'Well you'll be happy that I'm cutting across Archer's field straight down to the little hamlet, no roads.'

'Look Art, I don't mind driving you.' Matt calmed, it was true that he earned next to nothing but Arthur had given him one thing that had been missing for so long in his life, self-esteem.

'You can't

'Eh?'

'Miss Allmes insisted that I came alone, she said I was the only one that she could trust.'

'That's a bit odd isn't it? Maybe she has finally lost it. Isn't her sister there?'

'That's what I thought, she didn't mention her though. Anyway cash up front. I'll tell you what, how about a nice fish and chip supper on the business when I get back?'

Matt's stomach grumbled at the thought. He smiled at Arthur. 'Right you are chief, good luck.'

Arthur stumbled out and Matt was not to know that that was the last time he would ever see Arthur Jay alive.

2 THE COTTAGE

Arthur had not returned to the office that day and eventually Matt assumed he had taken the money to one of the various watering establishments around the town so, finding some money lying around, he locked up the office late and headed for the Crown Hotel for a hot, affordable meal which tonight was hot parsnip soup followed by battered haddock and chips with a pile of peas as garnish. Bess, the landlady, delivered his soup, thick and steaming. Bess was a bubbly woman of middle years, probably about fifty he hazarded a guess, in his head of course. Her husband, Darren Wilde, shouted across from the busy bar. 'Watch her Matt! She quite fancies anyone that adores her food. Look what she's done to me.' Darren produced a huge, smooth round belly from under his jumper; it was as hairless as his balding head. The bar flies propping up the bar cheered and whistled and they soon all carried on their own private conversations.

'Take no notice of them' Bess said in a soft Welsh lilt. She was a buxom attractive woman with long reddish brown hair and big brown eyes. 'No Arthur tonight then?'

'He hasn't been in then? I expect he'll find his way here sooner or later, he went up to Miss Allmes' house to do a job.

'What does that old cow want now? Trouble that one, tried to have me shut down for unhygienic food preparation the lot. I had the authorities all over my kitchens. Turned out she had done the same at The Anchor and The Tandoori Box restaurant, each time getting a free meal and gift voucher, not from here though, my Darren wrote her a letter. We barred her.'

'When was this?' Matt loved his little chats with Bess. It always kept him in the loop with village gossip, even though Wimborne was a town with a Minster it retained a certain village quality of times gone by that had attracted Matt to live there, well camp there, at the moment but he hoped to get proper roots in the town sooner or later.

'She tried it on here last Tuesday, yes a week ago today, spiteful old lady she is.'

'What about her sister? She was living with her wasn't she, hence the appearance of old Miss A and that ridiculous little black Poodle.'

Bess drew nearer almost thrusting her ample bosom around Matt's cheeks 'Well that's the thing, nobody has actually seen this sister, not sure where the story came from, all we know is that she now walks a poodle which presumably belongs to the mystery sibling and is more spiteful than ever.

'Yes indeed, well when I catch up with my boss tomorrow maybe he'll enlighten me as to the persona that is Miss A's sibling and I'll be right round to tell you Bess.'

'Oh you promise?'

'With food as good as this, how can I refuse?'

'You are a charmer Matt, extra lump of ice cream for your pudding.'

'I'm afraid I can't afford pudding tonight Bess.'

'I think it's on the house tonight for you Matt.'

Darren heard this and shouted again 'Watch it Matt. What did I tell you?' He slapped his tummy and once again the crowds cheered and laughed.

Matt loved this town. Getting divorced and moving here was the best thing he had done.

Matt was woken with a start when a heavy rapping on the side of his van echoed around him. After being fed and watered at The Crown Hotel the previous night, not to mention the usual permission to have a shower in one of the spare rooms, something Bess and Darren insisted he was welcome to do morning and night until he was solvent, he had gone back to his campervan for a good night's sleep, sleeping soundly until now. Bang, bang came the sound again, so slowly Matt stretched and wriggled across the floor and peered out behind the blinds. Two Police constables stood in waiting, one a rather tall skinny man whose uniform hung on him limply; the second was a WPC who was completely opposite, short and rather rotund, a uniform stretching at every seam. They both glared in that emotionless, we are your masters kind of way that would normally put the fear of God in people but not for Matt who just slid the door open and yawned while stretching his naked torso in front of them, his lower parts were covered by wrapped around duvet but it was enough for the steely glazed WPC to soften a little, her cheeks ever so slightly reddening.

'Mr Matt Powers?' the skinny giant asked.

'Hi Barry, you know it is, what's all the…' he mimics their stony faces and grunted '…about, someone die?' The moment he had said it he wished he hadn't. The pitbull of a woman with cheeks now as bland as the rest of her suddenly had him up against the van and in handcuffs at which point the duvet wrapped around his midsection dropped revealing bare buttocks.

The WPC screamed as though she had never seen such a sight before in her life.

'Barry what the hell is going on, at least let me get changed first.'

PC Barry Berry, whose parents obviously named him such because they wanted their son to be ridiculed his entire life, nodded and then turned to the little woman. 'Oh for God's sake, go wait in the car Beryl, it's only Matt, he isn't going to run.' WPC Beryl shuffled off like a scolded child. 'Sorry Matt, she's new to beat walking. Look, I'm afraid I'm going to have to take you in.'

'Doing your job mate, and I really want to know why but unless you let me get dressed, Bunty the butcher will be out here to nab my bits for her chopping board.' Matt turned round and swung his Penis to and fro, proving that he had ample proportions to lose.

PC Berry now blushed and nervously unlocked the handcuffs. Matt quickly grabbed some boxers, jogging pants and a sweatshirt before locking the van and following Barry to the parked Police car that sat with the glum looking WPC Beryl sadly staring out from the front passenger seat.

'Oh Baz let WPC Beryl take me in with the handcuffs back on if that's what she wants, look at that little…um poor face.'

'Matt, please call me officer or something, the Sergeant would give me a right royal rollicking if I was over familiar with prisoners and now with DCI Hepton taking charge.'

'Prisoners, Hepton? Why exactly am I being dragged in?'

Barry paused, 'Arthur's been found dead.'

Matt froze, mouth open 'What? Good grief, how, where?'

'Let's just get to the station eh?'

Matt got into the back of the Police car and the rest of the journey sat quietly, his brain racing with the few facts he already knew.

Wimborne Police station was a small but modern satellite community building. The interior was adorned in public information posters and an overabundance in pea green paintwork. Matt was shown into a small interview room that appeared to double as the canteen because several police staff shuffled quickly out with tea and donuts in hand as he, Barry and Beryl entered. Beryl tried to look as if she was in control of the situation and with mild amusement Matt noticed that Barry was letting her. He obviously had a soft spot for the WPC. Barry ushered Beryl out of the room then showed Matt to a seat by a desk.

DCI Charles P Hepton eventually entered the room to commence the interview. He sat opposite Matt behind the desk and, as the questioning went on, it soon became clear to Matt that they clearly didn't have him down as poor Arthur's killer, but was routinely crossing him off the suspect list, lucky that poor plump Beryl didn't bring him in in handcuffs then…

Hepton was a hard man, early fifties with an air of contempt about him, his greying hair was slicked back to cover a bald spot and with his beaky nose the whole look made him resemble a bird of prey. 'Tell me Powers, why exactly was Jay the drunk in the middle of Archer's field anyway?'

Matt thought for a moment. If he told them everything then they'd only get in the way. Art would have wanted the detective agency to solve this case, after all without Arthur's cash flow, such as it was, the agency would soon fold anyway. 'I know that 'Arthur' was off to visit someone, social like, but his business was his own…' he stated matter of factly before adding '…Hepton.' With a smile that infuriated the DCI.

'If I find that you are holding back vital information then I will have you arrested for, for…'

'Obstructing and withholding Police evidence.' PC Barry interjected from the corner of the room where he had been quietly standing almost to attention.

'I know, I know! It was a dramatic pause; don't they teach you anything at Police training these days?' Hepton said turning red and looking like someone had stolen his thunder.

'May I ask how he was killed?' Matt dared to ask, throwing the room into silence with a calm questioning face.

'He was strung up like a scarecrow, hands nailed to a cross.' Hepton found himself answering automatically

'Like a crucifixion then?' Matt pushed

Hepton suddenly came to his senses. 'I'll do the bloody questioning here Powers. For now you are dismissed but let me warn you, this is a murder inquiry which makes it a Police matter, do I make myself clear?'

'Perfectly chief, this is being dealt with by the Police, yes, even I can comprehend that.' Matt smiled his most winning smile again that only appeared to make Hepton redder so he thought it was best to vacate the premises pronto.

Out in the car park not long after, PC Barry caught up with Matt as he headed toward the High street. 'Matt, you will keep a low profile won't you? It's just, well old Hepton is a stickler and he despises self-appointed investigators.'

'Barry, how can I ignore this? Arthur was a friend. I'd hate to think where I would have been if I hadn't found his friendship.'

'But you live in a van, what favours has he done for you? He was a drunk.'

'Ok, I was down on my luck, some might say I still am but, well, that man gave me my self-esteem back, purpose. Do you know, my wife was having an affair with the vicar that married us even before we married? It has a lasting effect on a man let me tell you!'

'Mmm I had heard, you know, town gossip and things.'

'Blimey, well if they're all talking about me they're leaving some other poor sod alone.' Matt found it amusing that he was the talk of the town.

'Oh I shouldn't think so, the Bakelite Womens Guild has plenty of people to gossip about.'

'And you know this how?'

'Oh yes well my mum is a member. I tell you, if there is anything worth knowing then the Bakelite Womens Guild are one step ahead.'

'Really? Well I would love to meet these ladies. Do you think you could arrange it for me?'

'Oh, but I don't think...' Barry suddenly panicked that Matt was going murder hunting.

'Relax Barry, it's just to promote my business. If I need to survive on my own, then I'm going to have to speak to the heart of our town haven't I?'

'Oh right, nothing to do with murders then? Oh yes, good, ok. I'll speak to Mum and give you a call soon.' Barry walked back to the station.

From one of the Police office windows DCI Hepton had watched the two friends talking.

Later that day after getting washed in the Crown Hotel and fending off questions from Beth who, along with Darren had been questioned by the police and had been Matts main alibi, Matt stepped out of his van in a fresh set of clothes, a yellow t-shirt and green jeans, an ensemble of charity shop wear but beggars can't be choosers as his wife had ended up with the house in Poole and custody of Wilfred, their baby. Wilfred was a rusty coloured bloodhound. The thought of him being taken for walks by that bloody philandering vicar really cut him up but for now he had to manage his own situation. His camper van, charity clothes and a detective agency that will probably fade away, unless... well, a thought had raced through his mind, it made him feel a little guilty but maybe just maybe he really could solve the murder. Of course, he owed it to poor Arthur to solve it but to actually solve the case to promote the business? Now that would be genius.

The blue police tape was all around his van and the building that housed the agency. Poor Bunty would have been prevented from working at her Butchers shop today. I wouldn't want to be the Police officer who had to tell her that, Matt thought, just as WPC Beryl stepped out of Bunty the Butchers rear entrance still talking enthusiastically with Bunty. The two women were a rotund vision of womanhood with Bunty a good foot taller than Beryl. Matt watched with interest as Beryl was completely animated in conversation and Bunty, a usually ferocious but lovable gal was enjoying her company, and then they kissed.

Matt dropped his keys in mild surprise. Well, poor Barry was in for a shock he thought as he picked them up. That kiss was no peck on the cheek, still, good for them! He stood up as both ladies approached him, 'Bunty and WPC   Beryl,   nice   to   see   you   again.'

'I hear you've been flashing your sausage around Matt. I could do with something for the counter.' Bunty smiled devilishly

'You keep your Butchery to yourself you wicked cow.' He joked, noticing that even Beryl was enjoying the joke.

Bunty suddenly grabbed his crotch 'Mmm a few pounds worth there Matt. I could make a profit. You better lock that van tonight... oh' Bunty suddenly looked ashamed and cried, something she was not accustomed to. 'I'm so sorry Matt, saying something like that, poor Arty, who could have done such a thing?'

'Do you think you can help?' The little voice was sweet and for a moment Matt looked round to find out where it had come from before setting his eyes on Beryl.

'I'm sorry?'

'This murder, I shouldn't say anything, it's just that this DCI, everyone is falling about his blustering orders. I just think we need someone that can quietly get on with it. Bunty says you're the tops…' Beryl's cheeks began to redden again.

Still with tears in her eyes Bunty put an arm around Beryl, 'Don't tell him that Beryl, he'll think I like him.'

Beryl looked around nervously and pulled Bunty's arm away before giving her a peck on the cheek. 'Bunty please.'

'It's alright Beryl, Matts ok.'

'Do I take it you two ladies are acquainted then?' Matt cheekily asked. He then waved his hands 'listen Beryl, um, I mean Officer. Can I go up to the office, just to get a few of my bits? I promise I won't touch any possible evidence.'

'Oh well you're not meant to.'

'I promise you, I will get to the bottom of this but I just need to get my diary from the office, that's all.

'He's a man Beryl but a truthful one, a good'un.' Bunty stated.

'Be quick then, and don't touch anything.' Beryl said with an enthusiastic wave of her hand.

Matt pecked both ladies on the cheek then shot over to the side door that lead up to the office.

When he eventually returned to his parked campervan, no one was around, which was fortunate, he got in it and soon with engine revving, drove out ripping the Police cordon tape apart.

Just outside Wimborne sat the little hamlet of Horton Stoney. It consisted of twelve cottages once part of the Horton Grange estate, but sold off to pay for renovations up at the Old Grange itself. The Hamlet sat on a quiet country lane, the cottages lining the road on either side all semidetached and thatched. It was on this quiet lane that a yellow and white Volkswagen campervan drove onto, with a gentle putter. Matt had decided to drive to the cottage he believed Arthur had been renting. Taking the address from one of the many bills at the office he eventually pulled up in front of a sweet looking semidetached cottage with a well-kept garden. The home was on the right hand side of the semi, surrounded by a white picket fence and neatly established shrubs. The van parked in a parking area at the front of the cottage that didn't interfere with lane traffic, not that there was any, as the lane only led to one of the obscure entrances of the Grange itself and any visitors there tended to take the main drive which sat a mile further east.

Matt stepped out and immediately felt eyes peering from netted windows all around him. He braved it up the gravel path to the front door which had honeysuckle climbing up one side and drooping into the neighbouring garden. He looked over the outside, the curtains were closed. He then decided to brave ringing the bell. Someone was moving inside, I hope this is the right house he thought. Maybe one of his lady friends was living with him. He glanced into the next door garden which was bland but neat and tidy. Suddenly the door opened and he swung round once again today giving his most winning smile only to feel it drop from his face. DCI Hepton stood there with an eyebrow raised questioningly.

In the small cottage kitchen two uniformed Policemen stood over a seated Matt while Hepton paced before him. Matt began to laugh, there was barely enough room to breathe let alone pace the room. Hepton swung round and glared at him. 'What were my instructions to you, do you want to be arrested?'

'I'm sorry chief, he was my friend I can't just leave it.'

'How did you know anyway, I find it mighty fishy and it certainly gives you motive doesn't it eh?'

Matt had now totally lost the thread or point that Hepton was making. 'Sorry?'

'You will be. You being here is proof in my eyes. You can't deny that you didn't know hey? Get out of this one Powers.

'Now listen moosh, you are talking in a language I can't understand, so what are you on about?'

The two policemen shuffled nervously. Hepton scared everyone at the station and no one would dare talk back to the man, even prisoners, the few that they had would kowtow when the chief was in town but not Matt Powers who suddenly stood up and stared Hepton down.

'The will,' he blurted suddenly sounding unsure 'you must have known.'

'DCI, are you referring to Arthur's will? He had nothing to give, if he had a will, I would hardly be part of it would I?'

'B..but you are.' Hepton stuttered, he actually stuttered. Matt thought.

'Yeh right! What have I got, bottle of vintage whisky, some old tobacco? Matt looked around the small kitchen and for the first time something occurred to him that had clearly not registered when Hepton had dragged him from the front doorstep by the scruff of the neck, this kitchen was spotless, in fact everything was in a place, a proper place. 'Wait up, he didn't rent here did he? It's too tidy; you must have seen the office, Arthur lived his life in a complete mess there is no way he lived here.'

'Didn't know him well then, is that what you're stating?'

'Well it's been almost 6 months that I have worked for him, mainly keeping his business afloat, he liked to drink and had a few women on the go, not that I met any of them, oh I tell a lie, old Mrs Dingles at the post office, I know for a start something went on there for a while, we had free postage stamps for well over a month last December, that fizzled out come New Year though, so did the freebies.'

'Get a statement Cordy, radio in for someone to get it done today!' Hepton ordered to one of the constables standing by, who promptly shot off, probably glad to vacate Hepton's immediate area.

'They really jump to your tune don't they?' Matt chanced

'So will you if you know what's good for you Powers!'

'I would if you'd only tell me what is going on. I don't believe for a moment that you consider me the suspect, am I right?'

'Well I do consider you inept and yes, unlikely, but you are still a suspect.'

'Then why am I now getting the third degree?'

'Because smart arse, you are here!' Hepton declared shouting Matt into silence.

Hepton began to pace again, this time with more room to manoeuvre. Eventually Matt challenged him.

'Well are you going to tell me or what?'

'This cottage, it's yours. It seems old Arthur was holding back on you. The house, the business and all his assets belong to you. So you see Powers, that gives you motive, especially someone in your situation.' Hepton stuck out his chin in gleeful pride daring Matt to make his move.'

'You really are some dopey idiot Hepton, I was with a whole group of people last night, by the time I left their sight I can almost guarantee that poor old Arty was already dead. Yes, I have motive given that my wife has taken all things material to me, and I'm not talking Wilfred here.'

'Wilfred?' Hepton managed to get in.

'My dog, but you are forgetting what I told you, Arty was like a Dad to me, I'd no sooner harm him than any of my family.'

'Aha! What about your estranged ex-wife.' Hepton suddenly looked pathetic.

'Been doing your homework I see. I feel nothing for her, she left me...'

'For the Vicar yes, we've interviewed them.'

'You what!'

'Background, it's necessary in a case like this.' Check mate from Hepton, Matt sat back down, all deflated.

'Checked your last job too, got sacked for, now let me see, kiddie fiddling?'

The room suddenly turned cool, the remaining constable turned to Matt his face motionless and unfriendly. Hepton stopped pacing and drew himself up to his full height staring at Matt knowing he had won the conversation and character assassination.

'Why would you say something like that? The whole incident was a complete crush on the student's side and I was a teacher at the local college. The student was twenty years old, hardly a kiddie as you put it!'

'A boy too wasn't he?'

'A young man yes!' Matt looked from one man to the other.' Now look, he was having some emotional problems in his private life, he approached me for some advice, eventually he came to me every week asking for this or that…'

'And you gave him it too didn't you?'

'I gave him advice yes, eventually I realised that he had fixated an attraction on me and told him that I had asked one of the lady Counsellors to help him, that's when he reported me. I was proven innocent of course but was asked to leave…'

'Sacked.' Hepton sneered, enjoying this added baiting. The police constable now looked at Hepton with contempt, clearly having weighed the facts up and deciding Matt was ok, it didn't go unnoticed by Hepton. 'Once a rotten apple.'

'I'm going to report you Hepton, I am going to prove my innocence and see you get dragged over the proverbial coals.'

'Not if I lock you up first.'

'Did you or did you not say that I was not really a suspect? You keep going round in circles' Matt found his inner pride and decided enough was enough. 'I'll tell you what I'll do, do you see my mobile phone I am going to dial our Police Commissioner, like so' he dialled a number rapidly, 'I suggest you get back to your station because you're not talking to him on my allotted free minutes.'

'You don't know Commissioner Bavistock!' Beads of sweat bubbled up on Hepton's brow.

'What old Tubby, Nigel Bavistock went to the same golf club as me. Only last week I said, Tubby, the policemen really are getting younger these days, He turned to me and…'

'…Yes I'm sure it's all very drole but you don't really have to speak to him surely, I am only doing my job. Look, maybe I did go a bit too far, it's my way, break down the suspects and see where it takes you, with you I just needed to be sure.' Hepton was snivelling with such conviction that the police constable stood by him decided he had heard enough and left. 'Andrews, where are you going, get me the squad car from up the lane, Andrews!' Hepton looked back at Matt who had pocketed the phone away. 'Well thank you Mr um Powers, I can't let you remain here though sir, I'm sure you will be allowed to return once we've checked over the place.'

The winning smile returned to Matt's face. 'I quite understand Detective Chief Inspector. Thank you for your understanding.

They both left the cottage. Matt sat in the van and watched as the squad car emerged from further down the leafy lane and for a moment he thought that the two police officers in the car were about to drive on, leaving Hepton stranded but they obviously thought better of it, stopping at the last moment. Matt pretended to look at one of his outdated newspapers stealing a glance as

Hepton got in the car, Hepton looked across with a grimace trying to be a smile. Poor sod, Matt thought, he had just been outclassed by Matt Powers PI and soon to be owner of the business and this mysterious cottage. He looked at the neighbouring house, all the curtains were closed, obviously a weekend retreat or a holiday let.

'That be Jared Allmes' house.' Came a voice at his passenger window. Matt almost jumped.

'My God! You scared the living shite out of me.'

An old man stood there nonplussed, he wore a knitted woolen hat over grey matted curls, easily into his eighties. 'You were looking at the house next door, yes?' The old man had a strong Dorset accent.

'Did you know Mr Jay?'

'Dead is he, oh, oh that is a pity, he always looked after everyone around here, did all the gardens.'

'You're joking right? Arthur Jay, alcoholic, chain smoker and lock up your daughters' madam…'

'Don't be crude young'un. How was he killed?'

Matt got back out of the van, 'Look, you are right it was crude of me. Arty was a friend and I worked at his detective agency, he was, well someone strung him up on a scarecrow pole, I don't know yet how he was killed but I know I'm not going to rest till I find out, did you say the neighbour's name is Allmes?' All sorts of theories were flooding through his head, was this at last a lead?

'Aye lad, that it is.'

'Sorry, where are my manners, my name is…'

'Matt Powers, aye, Mr Jay often talked of you kindly, said you were a cracking tea maker.' The old man began to laugh which caused him to cough. 'Not bad at detective business either.'

Suddenly old people began to wander out of their homes and for a moment Matt thought he was on the set of a geriatric Wicker man film.

'I'm Wilfred by the way.' The old man finally offered up.

'Really, that's my dog's name.' Matt was conscious that he was pulling a crowd.

'Can he help, Wilf?' A plain woman asked from amongst the gatherers.

'I ain't asked yet woman have I?' The old man replied. Matt guessed that this was Wilf's wife.

'What's going on here?' Matt asked

'Well we get up early round here. Jeffrey over there often goes into town for his breakfast, we had already heard but didn't believe it about Mr Jays. We got a lot of respect uh, had a lot of respect for him. We want to hire you to find his killer.'

'But the police…'

'Are useless young'un, now will you do it?'

'Well, yes, that is to say I don't need your money, I'm going to anyway, Arty was good to me even though I was so totally wrong about who he was.'

The crowd began to laugh and giggle. An old lady who could barely see shuffled forward, her back permanently arched. 'He says you were none the wiser, he even watered down his whisky, it's how he fooled the town into revealing things, had 'em all fooled he did.'

'Obviously someone fooled him though. This Mr Allmes, where is he?'

'He's army boy ain't he!' Wilf stated. Comes back some weekends, nice lad, works in the hospitals, not been here for a fortnight now.'

'Is he anything to do with a Miss Allmes over North side do you know?' Matt tried to sound casual.

'That'll be tellin wouldn't it.' Wilf said before hobbling off, along with the rest of the Hamlet

Matt watched them all disperse. He was soon to inherit this cottage, and these were to be his neighbours but somehow he guessed that they already knew that.

3 JARED ALLMES

It was to be three weeks later that, sporting a black eye, the cottage came into Matt's possession. Up to that point he began his snooping, taking him to several places on the hunt for clues. Miss Allmes' cottage was the first port of call. The police were nowhere to be seen, which of course they wouldn't be as they had no reason for thinking that Arthur had been heading there on that fateful night to begin with.

The cottage was a sad shadow of its former self with broken tiles and cracked walls, the midday sun and clear blue skies doing nothing to enhance the property. Matt knocked the thick oak front door, the dreaded black poodle could be heard barking from within, after a moment a succession of bolts were drawn back and a gap in the door appeared.

'What do you want?' demanded the voice, no face had appeared behind the gap.'

'Miss Allmes, my name is Matt Powers, I am… sorry, I was, the junior member of Mr Jay's Detective Agency. I don't know if you've heard but I'm afraid he's dead, he was murdered.

'Serve him right, cat killer!'

'Yes well that's as maybe. I was just wondering if I may ask you some questions.' There was silence for a moment and Matt thought, given the chilly reception, that it was unlikely that Miss Allmes would welcome him in, but just then the door opened and in the dark old hallway stood Miss Allmes all in black with a netted veil over her face. It wasn't until they passed a sideboard that he noticed the veil matched the black lace doily under a plant pot. What was that all about.

Matt was shown to a small drawing room which housed two worn cloth high back arm chairs in front of a two bar electric fire. The décor was bland and brown. Miss Allmes pointed to one of the chairs as she sat in the other. The woman didn't seem her legendary ferocious self, even appearing subdued.

'Is everything ok with you Miss Allmes?'

'Yes, of course, why are you here?' snapped the veiled woman.

'You're looking well.' blast! Matt thought, did I really just say that? 'Wwhat I mean to say is, when I've seen you around town you tended to hobble.' Matt's speech dried up as Miss Allmes glared from behind the black lace doily just as the dreaded poodle began to bark again from further in the house. Matt decided to get to the point. 'Did Arthur Jay come to see you as requested three nights ago? I know he received your phone call and it was that night that he was murdered.'

'How did he die?' Miss Allmes offered in response.

'Well he was…Are you sure you want to know?'

'Might as well.'

This was some cold hearted old harridan, Matt reflected. 'Well, I'm sorry, I really don't want to go into detail…'

'No stomach for it then. Eh lad?'

'I really don't think…'

'I never rang Old Jay or whatever he calls himself these days, I would sooner gouge my eyeballs out than see that beast again, he killed my cat.' The old woman then began to babble utter nonsense.

Miss Allmes was losing focus and clearly not listening so Matt decided to make a hasty retreat. 'Yes well I'm clearly wasting your precious time Miss Allmes, I'll see myself out.' And with that, shot out the door as fast as he could.

Walking quickly to the parked campervan further up the road, Matt was left wondering why Miss Allmes would question why Arty would call himself anything other than Arthur Jay. Maybe it was just part of her eccentricities or maybe she had let slip a major clue. The other question was, could she be lying about telephoning Arthur and arranging that private meeting? If it wasn't her then it was most definitely his killer.

Matt decided a little surveillance was needed so drove his van up to Perrin's Wood which was well positioned to overlook Miss Allmes' cottage and was a well-known haunt for lovers and fans of the noble art of dogging. The trees of the wood gave way to a gravel track on the left, Matt drove slowly up the track and was pleased that there was only one car parked at the far end. Parking near the trees that would overlook the cottage he got out, momentarily scanning the car, a black Mercedes, very nice, no one was in it, dog walker most probably, Matt surmised then entered the wood. A figure in some undergrowth nearby observed quietly.

Four hours later Matt stood up from a clump of bracken that he had been sat in, bored with the view. It was perfectly situated high up the hill and beyond several fences to where the Allmes' cottage sat, but nobody came or went from it so he decided to head back into town. The Mercedes was still in the car park along with a Citroen people carrier and a large white van, which were both parked alongside his van. As he approached his trusty Volkswagen the sound of love making could be heard around the walls of the interior of the van, which had misted windows in its walled sides, Matt was just grabbing his keys when suddenly a pair of womens breasts slapped against the misted window squidging outward like a pair of bloated beach balls, Matt dropped his keys and on retrieving them could clearly see a nubile bleach blonde female and owner of said breasts smiling at him through moans of ecstasy. Matt froze as she whipped her long tongue out and whipped it round her equally over bloated lips. Matt quickly unlocked his van and got in just in time, as the side panel of the van next to his slid aside and there sat the couple in all their glory, she now faced the rear and screamed in delight as a brute of a man was taking her doggy style and facing him with a worrying glint in his eye.

The Volkswagen campervan left the car park with a wheel spin that blurred the area in a momentary haze, out of the haze the black Mercedes slowly followed.

Back on the open road Matt breathed a sigh of relief and began to laugh, 'What a world.' He shouted. On approaching Wimborne he became aware of the black Mercedes behind him, was it a coincidence? On slowing down in an attempt to see just who was driving the black car suddenly shot off down a side road. 'I'm seeing menace in my own shadow now.' Matt said to himself.

Matt was finally allowed back into the office in the days that followed so he began to hunt out any files that pointed to the work that Arthur was on, maybe someone had a grudge, truth is, the business didn't really have the kind of cases to merit revenge, lost and founds, the occasional cheating spouse case but the police were all over those ones and he was sure Beryl would keep him in the loop regarding those.

He opened the filing cabinet that contained the half opened whisky bottles; he stared at them for a moment then opened the lid of one to sniff. Yuk, it really was whisky, for a moment he had thought that it may have been all a big joke on Arthur's behalf, that maybe he had been hiding behind the pretence of being an alcoholic just to do his job but no, half-drunk bottles proved the theory wrong.

An envelope at the bottom of the drawer and under the bottles suddenly caught his eye. Matt slipped his hand under the whisky bottles and retrieved it. The envelope was sealed and addressed to himself, Matt found a letter opener from his own desk and forced an opening through the top, another sealed envelope was within and a note. This time the sealed letter was addressed to Jared Allmes. Matt raised his eyebrows in surprise. How curious. He quickly opened up the folded note that simply said – Dear Matt, so the buggers got me in the end, no problem, please ensure letter gets to said address. Art PS Have a drink on me.

The pit of Matt's stomach dropped, the old buzzard was going to be missed, it had finally hit him how much he would miss him. Matt handled the sealed note and weighed the paper opener in his other hand debating whether to open it or not, no, no it was Art's wish for it to be delivered and he was going to do it. Just maybe this Jared was connected to the murder.

Mrs Della Dingles set off to the church hall for the evening; it was the Bakelite Womens Guild weekly meeting that usually consisted of coffee, homemade cakes and gossip. Della Dingles was a smart woman in her fifties who tended to wear designer clothes that were paid for, not by the post office that she ran, but from her husband's local builders business. With an air of superiority constantly wafting from her in the form of expensive perfume she walked along the street like a queen on a jubilee walkabout.

Matt had received a phone call from Barry that day to inform him that he was more than welcome to attend their meeting that fine summer evening so it was quite by chance that onto the same street stepped a smart Matt Powers in jeans, a sleeveless burgundy jumper over a white t shirt. Despite the warning of perfume fumes the two visions collided.

'Oh, I am terribly sorry Mrs Dingles, I was miles away.'

'I do wish you'd look where you're going, honestly.' She scolded. Looking over herself with as much dignity and frozen glances as she could muster before finally concluding, 'Well, there doesn't appear to be any damage done.' She then smiled at Matt. 'It's you, Arthur's understudy.'

'Yes Mrs Dingles, how are you?'

'I'm perfectly fine thank you. Is that right that you are coming along to our little soirée this evening?' They began to walk on in the same direction.

'Yes, I'm coming along now. Do you think I can ask you a question?'

'Of course young man, ask away.'

'Well, it is kind of delicate.'

Mrs Dingles stopped walking again and looked at Matt. 'I see, yes well, better here than at home, my Brian got really annoyed when the police dragged the whole silly affair up again, I take it you are referring to dear Arthur's little dalliance with me?'

'Yes, yes I am. Did your husband get angry?'

'My Brian? Oh he was furious when he found out.'

'Prone to violence?'

'Now wait a minute young man…'

'I'm not that many years behind your age you know.'

Mrs Dingles suddenly showed great strength and willingness to reveal a more common side to her personality, as she suddenly pushed Matt up against a shop window and pointed a well-manicured finger in front of his eyes. 'My Brian works hard for us. He's not prone to violence so if you dare peddling your lies to anyone especially the police I'll rip your fucking nuts off and feed them to you, do we understand each other?'

'Perfectly well Mrs Dingles.' Della Dingles clopped off on her high heels leaving Matt watching her. '…Perfectly well.'

Further down the street a figure stood watching, the shoulders trembling as they contained mild amusement.

Matt decided to not attend the meeting after all. Clearly Della Dingles wasn't the lady she made herself out to be and her husband obviously had a temper, well who wouldn't when confronted with a cheating wife, they had obviously settled their differences but were either of them capable of killing. Admittedly Della recalled Arthur with fondness but that was moments before she channelled the she-devil.

On suddenly turning round to retread his route back to the van and probably the Crown Hotel bar he saw the figure of a man shoot out of sight. Matt broke into a sprint determined to find out who it was that didn't want to be seen. As he got to the side road he found it empty apart from a family busily getting out of a car, he slowly walked down the road which he knew would bring him near the Crown Hotel anyway, passing the family he heard the rev of an engine from a cut through lane then all of a sudden a black Mercedes shot out and sped away from him. 'I must be getting paranoid, surely not the same car.' Matt shook his head and continued on, he decided he wanted to be with his friends at the Crown now.

It was a lively night at the Crown. Barry was drinking there along with another girl, did he know about Beryl and Bunty then?

Hi Matt, how are you holding up? Oh this is Janice; she's just started in the police offices.

Matt smiled at Janice, who just looked down meekly, lifting her eyes towards him giving a little smile. Mmm another shy girl, it was clearly a turn on for poor Barry. 'Have you any leads Barry?'

'You know I can't discuss it Matt.'

'Come on mate, I need to know if you're getting anywhere, just for peace of mind really.'

'Well all I can tell you is that his family appears to be hard to track down. The DCI keeps his cards to his chest. I know a couple of titbits from the family past, Arthur's Mum had a baby exactly the same time as her best friend Isabel Padley, and when Arthur was older he worked in or near the old police station, doing what, I really don't know but as you can hear, I don't really have the gripping leads you want to hear. You must have blown Hepton's ego apart the other day, he went from being obsessed with your involvement, to not wanting to talk about you at all. I know you said something to him, Terry told me, he was the constable stuck with him at Arthur's cottage.

'I just told him that Commissioner Bavistock was an old golfing friend of mine.'

'You play golf then?'

'Not bloody likely! I once played a full round and putted around eighteen holes, I was useless.'

Janice took a noisy slurp finishing off her coke.

'Can I get you another coke Janice?' Matt asked but she just smiled and shook her head.

'No, we're both off to Poole for a meal at one of the fish restaurants Matt,' Barry said while putting on his coat. 'Tell me, how do you know the Commissioner then?'

'Read up his profile on Facebook didn't I. I knew that it would be handy knowledge to store away.'

At that moment Beryl came in with Bunty at her side. Barry caught their arrival and quickly made his excuses. 'Well see you soon Matt, must dash.'

'Ok Barry, nice to meet you Janice.' Janice smiled and a hand shot up and gave him very quick wave before they vanished out of the front door.

'Here he is, my big German sausage!' Came a bellowing voice in the busy crowd. Then Bunty appeared and slapped Matt on the back, Beryl followed close behind.

'Ladies, how lovely to see you again, and what would you want with my, um, German sausage, it's not as if you two would have a use for it.' Matt said in light-heartedness.

'You cheeky beggar, I'm a butcher remember!'

Matt put his hands up in mock surrender just as Beryl dived for a table and chairs, 'You eaten?' Beryl asked in a strong firm way that caught Matt off guard. He was beginning to think that she was quite meek but after meeting Barry's new girl anyone would appear assertive after Janice.

'I'm fine thanks Beryl, not really that hungry.'

'Then please sit with us for a bit?'

Wow, what had gotten into Beryl, she was confident and assertive.

'Forgive me for asking but have you got a more subdued twin?'

'No why?'

'I was just wondering what has got into you.'

'Do you mean apart from me?' Bunty butted in as they all took a seat around a small round wooden table.

'Listen Matt, I've done a bit of digging and found out that your boss was worth quite a bit of money, you should be getting the keys to the cottage tomorrow if old Hepton releases them.' Beryl said.

'Really? Well he's told me about the will Beryl, and he knows the cottage is bequ... bequee... to be mine so it's safe to assume it will be a fair while before I get to stay there, Hepton hates me, he's not going to hand those keys over just like that.'

'Well there's always the Commissioner.' Bunty joined in.

'How the hell do you know about that Bunty?'

'Doh, Beryl told me of course you Burk.'

Matt turned a questioning eye to Beryl and then realised 'Oh of course, now don't tell me, don't tell me, the boys have been talking back at the station, is that it Beryl?'

'Well yes, basically, is that ok?'

'What choice do I have? Do you know if Arthur has any relations alive?

'Not that I know, why?'

Just then Bess surfaced through the busy crowd, 'Here he is then. What's this I hear, that you have been holding out on me?'

'No. About what?' Matt defensively replied.'

'Well a little birdie tells me that beneath that messy exterior lays a well-tuned engine with a hell of a piston.' Bess pointed at Matt's body

'Ugh? Are you sure it was such a little birdie' Matt stated eyeing Bunty and Beryl.

'Oi cheeky!' Bunty said, slapping him across the head.

'It was me' Beryl confessed, her cheeks reddening.

'Well I guess it could only increase my street cred.' Matt winked. The three women sat looking at him expectantly. 'What?'

Bess smiled 'We just want to make sure you're ok Matt, you have friends here, you do know that?'

Matt could see the sincerity in all their faces, including Beryl who he had only known days. 'Thank you ladies, I do know that but honestly I am fine. Now if you don't mind it's getting a little bit like an American soap opera in here so I'll see you all laters.' He gave them all a peck on the cheek with Beryl's flushing crimson as Matt's lips approached for touch down.

As Matt approached the front door a burly, muscular gorilla in vest and jeans spun round on his chair. 'Hey Powers!' He spat with venom. All Matt remembered next was a fist like bloated sausages swinging straight at him, then he blacked out in the gentle arms of Morpheus.

Mick Dingles had just got off his mobile phone after a call from his wife. She had told him exactly what had happened in the street and that they needed to deter Matt Powers from poking his nose in where it wasn't needed, it was fortuitous then that said Matt Powers, was walking towards the exit of the Crown Hotel where Mick was drinking, and so in a blink of an eye he shot out and knocked the man out. He had one moment of shaking the stinging pain in his hand before Beryl flew through the air like an Olympic gazelle, well an athletic water buffalo would have been more apt; there was definitely something quite graceful about this rather large lady. She landed past the fallen Matt and was instantly in an attack position from some obscure oriental marshal art.

'Leave it out lard ass, I don't hit ladies.'

'Splendid, I can't lose, Hii-Yaa!' With that Beryl's hands flashed out on either side of Mick's head, knocking him out instantly. He slid down the side of the bar, a look of utter surprise froze on his face.

'And by the way, I'm no lady!' Beryl said with confidence, wiping beads of sweat from her brow, the bar room exploded with cheers and laughter.

'All right everyone settle down, nothing to see. What are you trying to do, get our license revoked?' Darren said as he and his wife filtered everyone away from the fallen. He asked a couple of his regulars to give him a hand with the dazed Mick and between them managed to sling him out the back entrance onto the bins area of the car park. 'That's where we keep the trash sunshine and by the way, you're barred!' Mick stood up and stumbled off; managing a two finger salute as he was joined by three of his friends who had sheepishly crept out the pub to see where he had been taken.

Inside the pub Matt now sat smiling, hearing how Beryl had come to his rescue. 'Off duty Police woman in bar room brawl, you are so busted if this gets out.'

'I will be if Hepton hears it involved you.' Beryl Laughed.

Bunty was well made up with her girl, 'I'm so proud of you baby, special treat for you later.'

'I can't wait.'

Bess appeared again with a nice hot cup of tea. 'There you go gorgeous, sweet tea, just what the doctor ordered.'

'Any biscuits Bess?' Matt gave a cheeky grin.

'Don't push your luck Private Dicky, I can still bar you don't you know. She gave him a peck on his head then shoved a pack of frozen peas across his face for the quickly forming black eye.

Matt kept a low profile the next few days, his eye went from pulsing red/brown to the usual blackening. Then one evening, just before locking the agency office up, there was a knock at the door.

Matt quickly sat down behind his desk, Arthur's old desk to be precise. The room was now incredibly tidy and the addition of an old bookshelf that had belonged to Bunty sat against the wall sporting all the case files in alphabetical order, all eleven of them.

'Come in.' Matt shouted as cheerful as he could sound without sounding simple.

The door creaked open and Mr Lance Embridge from Embridge, Embridge and Jones, Wimborne solicitors entered. Lance was the younger Mr Embridge, a handsome man in his forties who clearly looked after himself. He eyed Matt once over, then stopped at the black eye. 'Good evening Mr Powers, hope you're keeping well?' His left eyebrow lifted questioningly and once again his eyes looked Matt all over.

What the hell was this guy on? Matt thought and decided to copy him and starting at the feet studied Lance's shiny patent black shoes and then his neatly pressed black trousers that matched his jacket and waistcoat which had the last button undone, up to his burgundy black tie and neat brilliant white shirt which at this point matched the solicitor's brilliant white teeth that were bared in a humorous grin, followed by that bloody lifting eyebrow again.

'Can I help you, Mr Embridge isn't it?'

Lance was overjoyed that Matt knew his name and stepped right up to him. 'You have no idea how happy that makes me knowing that you know who I am, and just to think now I know what you know as I know what we are.'

'Eh?' Matt was lost 'What do you know, I mean I know what you know or was it, you know what I know?'

'You know…' Lance Embridge added as his hand slid up trying to find Matts nipple under his t-shirt.

'No, no, no, well I didn't till now and what you think you know is a no-no so please go get a cold shower or something!'

'Oh the teasing type eh?' Lance's voice hardened as he opened his jacket and produced a set of keys and a piece of paper. 'Trouble with you closeted types, you play the game then cry wolf.'

Matt stood mouth agape not really knowing what he had done, then it dawned on him that he had just mimicked eyeing him up and down. 'Oh I'm so sorry, you mean when I looked you over, sorry I was just…'

'Sign here please.' Lance stated producing a quality ink pen, now projecting a completely uninterested persona.

Matt didn't know what to say, 'Look, you're a good looking guy and all…'

Lance face beamed the brilliant white tombstones in his direction again.

'But!!' Mat quickly added as he could see that look in Lance' eye again, 'I'm sorry I am just not wired that way.'

Lance pulled back on the hopeful grin, this time managing a gentle smile; he then produced a set of keys. 'That's what they all say, ok Tiger, your loss. These are the set of keys to 18 Grange View, Horton Stoney as owned by Arthur Jay. Congratulations it is now yours. There is a matter of Mr Jay's finances so perhaps you could come into our offices in the next week?'

'Money, for me?'

'I can't say anything at this precise time, all I can say is that it would be beneficial to you Matt Powers, very beneficial indeed.'

Matt blindly signed the document his head swimming. Had he ever really known Arthur Jay?

'I'll see myself out.' Lance said giving Matt one more look over. 'Are you sure you don't fancy a…?'

'Positive.' Matt smiled feeling surprisingly flattered.

Lance shrugged. 'Look, you're not going to mention my little um…'

'Not a word, just proves what great taste in men you've got.' Matt joked almost regretting it.

Lance perked up ever hopeful 'Really?'

'Go!' Matt demanded, so Lance shrugged again and went with a smile. For a moment Matt stared at the keys in his hand. The cottage was his 'Bloody hell.'

The next day the campervan once again pulled into the quiet lane which was Horton Stoney and, as Matt drove up to 18 Grange View, his new home he was shocked to see a car parked outside the neighbouring cottage, a black Mercedes.

There was no sense of the neighbouring cottages curtains twitching but Matt guessed they were there stuck to their windows. He walked up the path, one eye on his neighbour the other on his own front door. He could hear nothing; maybe he could do the old sugar bowl trick once he'd settled in. As Matt released the lock of the front door and passed the threshold, waves of sadness hit him and as he stood in the hallway, a single tear paved the way to floods of tears. 'You stupid old buzzard, look what you've made me do.' Through his tears Matt began to laugh. 'Have a drink on me Arty, wherever you are.' Composing himself he decided to explore the cottage. From the hallway straight ahead sat the tiny kitchen; that much he did know. The stairway to his left was in dark wood and the door opposite was presumably the lounge/sitting room. Matt swung the door open to reveal a lovely room in darkness. He strode across and pulled back big heavy curtains to the front window that lit the room up. A plain coal fire sat on the wall that adjoined his neighbour, the furniture was all in situ and no alcohol bottles in sight. The furniture, two chairs and a sofa suited the cottage style in a comfortable way, the room even sported a nice wooden beam across the centre of the ceiling. Matt then pulled back the curtains at the other end of the room to reveal French doors on to a wooden patio area overseeing a beautiful well established garden.

'Wow, I wasn't expecting that.' He said to himself, or was he verbalising it for Arthur's sake, wherever he may be. He checked his keyring and guessed that one of his keys would fit the French doors. He was right and soon the pair of doors were swung open to reveal bird song and radio tunes.

Over the high fence could be heard Lady Gaga, no doubt the mystery stalker was sun bathing or something. For a moment Matt stood thinking and then acted out the idea of going upstairs to see if the bedroom window could reveal his neighbour.

There was only two clear windows to the back and they were the spare room, a small box room perfect for a study and the, a bath/shower room with a floral shower curtain and matching roller blind that covered a frosted glass window with a small upper opener. This was the window with the best outlook of the neighbour.

'You are kidding me?'

Putting a foot on the toilet seat and another on the side of the bath he lifted himself up and then first retracting the blind with its single central cord and then opening the upper window as quietly as he could manage, he squeezed his face up to the open space. The fence to his neighbour was tall but Matt could just make out a pair of bare feet resting on the end of a sunbed, the partially visible legs were hairy, either they were a man's' or the set of pins belonged to a carefree and gut wrenching hairy woman. One foot began tapping along to a song on the radio. Then suddenly the feet vanished and a man was standing just clear of the fence his back to Matt's spy post. The man was naked. Through the shock of suddenly seeing pert brown man buttocks, Matt lost his footing and plummeted into the bath taking the roller blind and shower curtain with him.

Matt lay in the bath screwing his face up in embarrassment, covered and wrapped in floral design print, if his neighbour remotely suspected what he had been doing then he'd be branded a pervert, all the trauma of the college incident flashed over him, haunting his memories like wild taunts. He became aware that the garden was quiet, the radio was switched off, just a coincidence surely, after all, the man had just stood up, maybe he was going indoors. Given that the radio was playing, the man probably didn't even hear Matt doing a triple summersault into an empty bath.

Just at the point where Matt had rested his demons in his head, convincing himself that his neighbour hadn't even noticed, the doorbell rang. Matt's stomach lurched.

As Matt opened the front door, shower curtain complete with floral print in hand, he found a tall swarthy looking gent with a strong firm brow, light grey/blue eyes and thick brown hair, high and tight at the sides standing looking at him with a bright cheery grin, dressed only in a burgundy cotton dressing gown, well-tanned and in his prime, late twenties early thirties, Matt surmised.

'Hi there neighbour, I heard a bang so thought I'd come and check on you. Are you ok?' The man said with a lively enthusiasm with an edge of humour, had this smiling invader realised what Matt was doing? Oh God, the humiliation.

'Uh, yeh I'm fine, I just,' Matt lifted the shower curtain 'well it's floral d'you see um... Matt had lost the ability to speak, why was he so embarrassed. Just then his head began to swim and, as if in slow motion, he floated to the floor with the merest of a notion of his neighbour catching him then blacked out.

Matt woke in a room not unlike his new cottage but in reverse. He lay on a leather studded sofa a matching chair was across from him, he was aware of talking then from what he presumed was the kitchen came a large round man with greying hair and beard to match looking at him from over his glasses

'Here he is, just rest my boy I'm Doctor Elmsgrove. It appears you're a little concussed...'

Matt went to speak but Doctor Elmsgrove stopped him

'...Now don't try to speak just rest, baths are hard nasty objects to fall in, I've checked you over, you're ok just a little concussed, I would recommend a night in hospital just to make sure?'

'No way.' Matt said as firmly as he could, he had a loathing for such places and tended to avoid them like the plague.

'No, I thought not, well it's jolly good that you have such an understanding neighbour and a model citizen too. Mr Allmes has insisted that you stay with him for a couple of days, he's well qualified to see you through it but any relapse and you'll be sent straight to hospital ok?'

Matt looked up as his vision began to blur.

'Just rest now Matthew. I'll check in a couple of days. Cheerio.' With that the Doctor let himself out.

Matt scanned the silent room again. Where was this Mr Allmes? There was a wooden clock above the fireplace, the time was eight, eight pm in the evening. He'd better get back home. He forced himself to stand and suddenly the room began to spin.

'Hold it there soldier,' a strong voice said as suddenly Mr Allmes appeared at his side and eased him back onto the sofa replacing the blanket, tucking it around Matt with care and concern. 'Listen to me Matt, I'm a medic in the army, you are in safe hands, just relax for now yes?

Matt had no choice but to relax 'OK' he simply said as he felt his whole body ease and the tension slipped into sleep.

The smell of coffee and burnt toast made Matt wake with a glint of sunlight searing through the tapestry styled curtains to the front of the house. Matt tested a foot out beyond the blanket that covered him, it was bare, he peered under the blanket, he was in his underwear, when did he undress? He thought.

'Your clothes are on the chair Matt. I hope you don't mind, you were well out of it so I undressed you. You took a nasty fall though I think.' Mr Allmes looked questioningly at him, a merest hint of that smile again.

'Ah yeh, the bathroom... what's the time?'

'It's 10am; I've made you some coffee and toast.' This Mr Allmes was friendly, was it all an act?

'Oh well thank you, Mr Allmes is it?' Matt asked, testing him and not wanting to presume.

'Come on Matt call me Jared, I'm sure you've been told about me, nothing is kept quiet around these parts.

'Really?' for a moment Matt thought about challenging him regarding Jared's car looking like his stalkers, but eyeing the questioning man with the happy go lucky smile standing in front of him and he himself feeling hungry, Matt conceded that there was a time and a place, eat first, answers later.

The room was soon bathed in sunlight as the curtains at either end of the room was drawn and hot coffee and a pile of toast was put before him on a tray. Jared pulled his chair right up to Matt and sat with a cup looking without saying anything, finally Matt sat back and looked him straight in the eye.

'Are you related to Miss Allmes?'

Jared's eyebrows raised as a smile broke out 'You knock yourself silly in your bathroom, out cold for quite a while and that's the first thing you ask me?'

'It's my profession.'

'Yes, so I have come to see…' Jared let the words hang, 'Do a lot of snooping do you?'

Oh God, he had seen him in the bathroom, what does he say to that? Luckily he didn't have to.

'No doubt you've clocked the car?'

'So that was you up at the woods and in the high street.'

'Well I had my reasons. It was by pure coincidence that you drove up to the woods. Were you checking on Miss Allmes place?'

'Yeh, how did you know?

'Well you were either there for that or a bit of dogging and as I witnessed you handle both I certainly know which you're more proficient at.'

'No, no, no I wasn't dogging, God forbid, I really didn't know!' Matt protested, feeling his face flush.

Jared put a hand up to Matt's bare shoulder, squeezing it gently. 'It's ok Matt, I was joking. I am a kind of relative to Miss Allmes, in an estranged way.'

Matt pulled himself away as he realised Jared had kept a hand on his shoulder. 'So why were you up at the woods?'

'Would you believe dogging?' Jared smiled but this time a defensive shield lay behind his eyes.

Maybe this man was somehow involved and here Matt sat with only his underpants on, eating what could be poisoned toast.

Matt jumped to his feet, a little wobbly but quite stable. 'Look I think I should return home, the last thing I want to be is a burden.'

Jared stood up and stood a little taller than Matt and emphasised it by stepping up to Matt, looking almost eye to eye with little space between. 'Arthur was a dear, dear friend of mine Matt, I know you suspect me but…' Jared paused and began to look across Matt's face before returning to eye gazing, 'I want to help Matt, nothing more nothing less.' He tilted his head to one side, the eye brow lifted and he smiled warmly.

This guy loved smiling, Matt thought. 'O-of course,' was all Matt could say as they both stared silently at each other. After what seemed like ages Matt backed over to chair where his clothes were piled up. 'I need to go to the Post office in town.'

'You can't drive!' Jared stated with an air of authority.

'I have to, times now wasting; I've not even settled in next door yet.'

'Well how about you get 'settled' and I'll drive you anywhere you need to go, remember, I need to keep an eye on you for now, concussion is a serious thing.'

Matts head began to buzz 'Ok, ok you drive me.' Matt felt his stomach leap with excitement. Whoa, what is that about? He thought before turning and leaving via the front door.

Arthur's belongings were all in situ around the cottage and it was a difficult thing to comprehend, everywhere Matt looked were ghosts of the man he had come to respect although looking at how neat and tidy this man was, he was pretty sure that he never really knew him at all. Maybe this was the place to start looking for clues. Matt decided to stay put so returned next door by hopping over the low fence that divided the neighbouring property and rang the doorbell.

The door opened and this time Jared was standing in close fitting boxer shorts and nothing else.

'Do you always walk around with nothing on?' Matt said feeling uneasy.

'Why, have you been spying on me?' Jared said, once again with that smiling expression.

Like poor old Beryl, Matt could feel his face flush, this guy is constantly embarrassing me, why oh why! So, it was obvious he had known that he was being watched yesterday, so what!

'Look Jared, I'm going to stay home and settle in, maybe venture out tomorrow if you want to travel to town, I have to see the solicitor. By then I'll be able to drive myself.' Matt said

'Well ok, it's probably best, I'll check in with you later though, just to make sure yes?' Casually Jared scratched at his underwear.

Matt just watched then shook himself out of thought. 'Yeh well, see you later then.' He suddenly remembered the sealed letter in his pocket which was addressed to Jared, 'Oh, this was to be given to you from Arthur, it's sealed, I haven't looked at it…' Matt sounded defensive.

That smile on Jared's face spread even wider. 'Of course not.'

With that and feeling embarrassed, Matt rushed back over the fence completely confused.

Jared watched him hot foot it back to his home and shaking his head in mild amusement. He decided he liked this Matt Powers just as Arthur had always said he would.

4 MURDER AT THE TOWER

Mick Dingles was a suspicious man, his wife was a loving woman and had a lot of love to give but sometimes, just sometimes she would expand her territory beyond their marital bed. He was no saint, in fact quite often when working far from home, he had a habit of picking up girls from bars and taking them to his hotel, finding the whole thing sleazy and sexy without the commitment, but on returning home he could dismiss that as purely business and leave it at that. As far as his wife was concerned though, she belonged to him and was expected to stay true, she didn't of course. First it was old Mullins who owned the Butchers before Bunty took over two years previous, then there was Arthur Jay himself, Mick found out about the affair via some loose talking on a local building job just before last Christmas. The careless plasterer ended up head to toe in plaster himself stating that he had fallen from the scaffolding, but nobody dared question him about it. To everyone's dismay, Arthur Jay was never confronted about the affair to the best of all the gossipers' knowledge. The affair ended and even Della Dingles looked nonplussed about there ever being one. Arthur and Della were never mentioned in the same breath again but, of course, now he was dead, but there was a secret, something that on this occasion both Della and Mick shared.

DCI Charles P Hepton paced the interview room as Mick glowered at the man. 'You can't chuffin well keep me ere against my will.' He had thought of complaining about that little fat police woman bitch that had attacked him in the pub a while back but decided against it, assuming he would become a laughing stock if more people heard about it.

Hepton stopped pacing and lent forward to him across the desk

'Oh yes I fucking can matey boy so you had better start talking. Do you or do you not know about the affair that your wife had with Mr Arthur Jays?'

'Nope.'

'Are you sure? You see, we have a statement from one Peter Holleringshaw stating that you had attacked him on the scaffold of a building site, resulting in him being pushed off.'

'Lies and jealousy, he envied me. He fell off that scaffolding; ask any of my mates, I was nowhere near him.'

'Yes, your mates would say anything that you wanted wouldn't they? Lead by fear Mr Dingles, do you?

Mick wasn't scared by Hepton, but it was a long time since he had been spoken down to like this, this man was going to pay for that.

'I want my lawyer present.'

'So you are hiding something then?'

'Don't try that one, I'm saying nothing till you get me a lawyer, geezer.'

'How eloquent Mr Dingles, a solicitor will not be necessary, you're free to go… for now!'

'I'm gonna report you, do you know that?'

'Yes I'd rather thought you might, only do hurry before I arrest you won't you?'

'Piss off.' Mick added before being led out.

Hepton stood pondering, he had hoped this particular hard nut would crack; perhaps the wife would yield to the interview technique. 'Barry!'

PC Barry Berry ran in. 'Yes sir?'

'Get me the file on Mrs Della Dingle.'

'S,she hasn't got a file sir.' Barry stuttered.

'Then bloody well make one, I have a funny feeling about these two.'

'Of course sir,' Barry added subserviently and vanished

Jared went out. Matt had just made some pancakes and had planned on inviting him round, the man had come over a couple of times in the afternoon just to check on Matt's eyes and blood pressure, he really was qualified at health stuff, Matt thought. Jared didn't really make much conversation and Matt began to think that maybe he had said something to upset his neighbour, on top of spying on his naked sunbathing. To make amends for looking after him, Matt had gone overboard with the amount of pancakes and was determined to not take no as an answer, that's when he had heard the neighbouring door slam and so ran to the front window to see the Black Mercedes wheel spin off. For a moment Matt considered trying to take chase but what was the point, besides, now he had a quiet evening of stuffing himself stupid with pancakes to look forward too, oh boy!

The early summer evening was warm. Della made her way up to Horton tower, casually strolling along the grassy path, her floaty white summer dress swimming in the gentle breeze.

Ahead stood the imposing eighteenth century gothic folly, stretching up to the blue evening sky, Della happily hummed a tune as she finally reached the base of the brick folly, only to find that she was alone. From the top of the hill she could see if anyone approached, it was deserted so she decided to walk around the base of the tower. 'Jared, Are you here?' she called, making her way awkwardly across the uneven turfs.

She eventually made it round to the door of the tower which was always locked these days, except it was actually slightly ajar. Gently Della pushed at the paint blistered old door to find a man standing there smiling cruelly.

'Jared, you scared me half to death, what a wickedly delicious place to have a little rendezvous darling.' Della bleated on while Jared stared with a smile so cruel. 'Come on darling, you said you'd give me something for my trouble.'

'I did indeed my dearest,' Jared finally said and spun Della around so she faced the doorway and from behind he gently kissed her neck. 'Tell me my sweet, has that Matt Powers been to see you yet?'

Della was mesmerised as Jared's gentle petting dried her mouth as a sexually charged spasm shot up her body. 'Mm Mick took care of him, he'd come to ask me something in the street but I sent him off with a flea in his ear.'

Jared suddenly stopped. 'What? I told you not to draw attention.'

'I haven't my darling, he thinks it's all to do with the affair, you know jealous husband. The Police had Mick in for questioning but he could handle it, they know he's got a short fuse, they even think the affair was true. Nothing they do will connect the dots.'

'Unless this Matt Powers should choose to interfere.'

'What him? That Happiness Detective Agency can't even save missing pets. I'm telling you, the Police have nothing to pin us.'

Jared began kissing her neck again, 'No but I have a succulent way of throwing them further off the path.'

Della was too aroused to bother asking, her eyes shut. If she had them open then she may have had a chance, but Jared made it a quick slice across her neck with a blade. Blood poured from the wound, colouring her pretty white summer dress, his gloved hands pushed her body to the floor before exiting the Tower and shutting the door on her dying body. Apart from a brief gurgling sound the Tower fell into silence.

Matt was asleep, not on the bed. He found that he just could not get into a dead mans bed so fell asleep on the tattered sofa in the lounge. The old clock on the mantel piece struck eleven causing Matt to slightly stir in the darkness, just then he heard a car pull up outside. His eyes opened wide and once again he found himself cracking a gap in the curtains to look out. Jared was walking up his garden path and suddenly stopped, it was hard to see in the half-light but, oh God he was looking straight at his window. Matt ducked back, surely he couldn't see him peer through the tiniest of peep holes, besides, he was only being a good neighbour.

'Matt, are you up?' came a whispering voice from the other side of the curtain.

What should I do? Matt thought to himself in a panic.

'Matt, please…'

Jared sounded seriously in need. Matt strode over and turned a lamp on, he realised that he had been sleeping without anything on so quickly wrapped the duvet around himself before heading for his front door. Sliding back the bolts he opened his front door to find Jared, blood dripping down his forehead, without hesitation it was Matts turn to take control, so shutting the front door he ushered an unsteady Jared into the lounge losing his duvet in the process, within seconds the naked Matt flew from kitchen to the seated Jared bathing a head cut with disinfectant and water.

'What happened to you Jared? You're dizzy too, did you crash or something?'

'No, I was watching the cottage, Miss Allmes' place, someone jumped me.'

Matt stood from his kneeling position, looking down to Jared. 'Then you are mixed up in all this? I knew your name wasn't a coincidence,' Matt's mind raced before he slowly asked his next question. 'Did you kill Arthur?'

Jared was silent, in fact he was not looking up at Matt, his eyes were lower, much lower.

For the first time Matt realised that he was standing naked and waves of self-consciousness swept over him. 'Oh yeh, sorry shall I…?'

'…Yeh' Jared said quickly.

Matt rushed off and eventually appeared in a pair of underpants and baggy T-shirt with bugs bunny on.

'Nice,' Jared mumbled

'Tell me Jared, did you k…

'No, I did not, I wouldn't he's…'

The silence lasted an age before Matt challenged him.

'He's what exactly? Matt's mind raced. He found himself thinking the unthinkable. 'Oh God, were you and him really close?' he found it difficult to verbalise just what he was thinking.

'You could say that yes,' was all that Jared would offer up.

'Oh I see, well good yeh, no what I mean is yes, it makes sense.'

'Eh?' Jared didn't know what he was getting at and put it down to the fact that they had both banged their heads recently. 'Look Matt, I do have to explain something to you but I think it best that you speak to Embridge, Embridge and Jones.'

'The solicitors, what do they have to do with it?'

'Look mate I'm going home to bed, just go talk to them yes?' Jared moved fast and was at the door before Matt had chance to protest.

'Jared, please don't go.'

Jared turned and smiled at him, cocking his head to one side he sucked air through his mouth. 'You need to be careful Matt, I get the distinct feeling you could be in trouble.'

'I wasn't the one caught snooping…' Matt knew this was the one statement he should have avoided as soon as he said it.

Jared smiled and as he went out the door said. 'Really? Well actually I'm not the habitual snooper am I? If you needed to see me sunbathe naked you only had to ask, y'know. I'm sure I'd find a window for you, oops did I mean window, no I meant I'm sure I could always find time for you.' With that said, Jared winked and set off for his own front door before Matt could retaliate, not that he could find anything to justifiably say and so stood mouth open, looking like a goldfish. Eventually shutting the door, Matt lent against it and began to laugh, Jared made him feel good, nothing tangible, just happy, but could he really have been in a homosexual relationship with Arthur Jay?

Surely not, Arthur wasn't gay, but if anything, the last few weeks had definitely proved that he really didn't know Arthur Jay at all, but if they were 'lovers' why was the house and whatever else, being left to himself and not to Jared? Maybe that was the motive for Jared being the real killer of Art? And what was the connection with Miss Allmes? Before too long Matt was fast asleep, dreaming of ballroom dancing. One moment with his ex-wife the next, with Jared in his arms…

Matt woke with a start, sunlight was searing behind the curtains. The morning was young and he had much to do.

It was a dog walker that found the body. Just after sunrise, Ronald Babbercomb walked Rusty his faithful dog up past the Horton Tower only to find Rusty running to the doorway and clawing and whimpering. Ronald realising that Rusty wasn't coming, made his way to the tower entrance and chanced the door handle. The body was soaked in blood and Ronald reacted instantly grabbing for his mobile phone in his coat pocket.

The police had the Tower cordoned off within half an hour, searchers had found the knife in some bushes down the track very quickly and had linked it to the murder within forty minutes and the local Police could identify the body and arrested the husband Mr Mick Dingles within the hour.

'Police work at its best wouldn't you say Blake?' Hepton boasted to his underling. They both stood back as men and women swarmed the tower for further clues.

On this bright early morning it was unfortunate that Matt had decided to have a little drive out in his campervan and even more so as it took him down the road near the tower walk. The amount of police presence drew his attention instantly and never one to hold back, he simply parked up and made his way towards the gate where even so remote and early a morning had drawn a sizable crowd.

The crowds annoyed Hepton, Blake wasn't surprised, everything annoyed Hepton but as they walked towards the gate Hepton suddenly exploded, shouting out in anger. 'Powers, get your ass here now!'

The crowd seemed to part leaving Matt standing, looking like a sheepish Moses at the Red Sea.

'DCI Hepton, how lovely to see you.'

'I want a word with you, walk with me!'

The uniformed police officers keeping the public out looked from Matt to DCI Hepton who nodded, they allowed Matt through.

Hepton looked at Matt and shook his head. The man was dressed in three quarter length shorts and only a waistcoat covering his chest that looked suspiciously like curtain material.

'I don't follow fashion DCI so don't give me that Vivian Westwood look.' Hepton just glowered. 'What's happened here then?'

'Murder you idiot, and I would find it most helpful if you could answer a few questions for me?' Hepton grinned bearing his teeth like a wolf.'

'Here we go again.' Was all that Matt could throw back to him.

Hepton took him up to the body. Now don't touch anything, do you recognise her?'

'Oh it's a dead body.'

'Well it's not Guy Fawkes night is it?'

'Yes well I know that, it's just not every morning I'm presented with – A DEAD BODY!' Matts cool finally breaking

After a moment Matt realised who he was looking at, 'Della Dingles?'

'Yes indeed, now we have her husband in custody, I understand that you and he had a disagreement not so long back?'

'Yeh, I think it was to do with me trying to ask his wife some questions about Ar...' he fell silent at Hepton's cold stare.

'So you are interfering in police business?'

'Oh come on Hepton, what do you expect me to do, sit back and watch the killer get away with it?'

'I expect you to stay safe.'

'I don't deny that this whole business is getting darker, I'm sure this has some bearing on Arthur's death but... hello that is odd.' Matt scanned one side of the small tower room and then the opposite side where the body lay. 'Why have you moved the body?'

'Don't be stupid, we haven't't' Hepton said, sounding most put out.

'Well someone has, look' Matt pointed to an area where the ground was just dirt a small tarpaulin lay half covering a patch of red dirt, Matt went to pull it back, looking across to Hepton for permission, Hepton nodded so Matt pulled back the Tarpaulin with the aid of a pen he had in his pocket, to reveal a tree branch with blood on it, he looked back at Dell's prone form with her neck clearly slit. 'The deed was done here but for some reason the body was moved hours later to that corner.'

'How could you possibly know that?'

'Obvious, all the blood is over here by the tarpaulin, where Della is now has no blood on the ground so she was moved when it had all...' Matt waved his hand around the neck area. 'You know, dried up a bit, whatever the medical term is.' Matt knelt nearer the log. 'Not sure what this is though, was she knocked out first?'

Blake stepped forward, 'No sir, what I mean is the only fatal injury was to the deceased's neck, no head trauma'.

'Don't sir him Blake, you'll be making him tea next!'

'Oh lovely, milk and two please...' Matt said as he walked over to the body, Hepton was about to bluster again but Matt continued 'The husband has been fitted up for it then?'

'I think not Powers, he's banged to rights, as we say in the force. The man has a temper and a jealous disposition, the murder weapon has been found down the lane, it's a knife from their kitchen.' Hepton sounded proud.

'No…'

'What?'

'This is such a setup, I'm sure he may know something but he didn't orchestrate this, the man's a moron.'

'You're a lousy detective, Powers. Leave it to the professionals yes?'

'That branch has definite bits of skin on it.' Matt found it easy to ignore Hepton while thinking deeply, 'Maybe she tried to defend herself…' A sudden thought occurred to him, Matt recalled his late night nursing stint washing the bloodied head of Jared Allmes. 'I need to go,'

'Oh you do, do you?' Hepton wasn't going to make this easy.

'You know I'm not a suspect Hepton so just leave off the bastard act.'

'Oh it's no act Powers.'

'Definitely not' Blake agreed laughing.

Hepton turned and gave one of his glares in Blake's direction, then looked back to Matt. 'Just go Powers, you're giving me ulcers, just stay out my way.' Hepton and Blake followed Matt out and watched as he walked down the grass track to the gate.

'Keep an eye on him Blake.'

'You don't trust him?'

'I do actually,' Hepton smiled 'The idiot is annoying and nosey, somewhere along the way he is going to stumble into the path of our killer and I'd hate for him to be the next victim, more than my reputation's worth, unfortunately.'

Blake just shook his head.

5 GOSSIP

Matt drove the campervan as fast as he could back to the cottage, what was he going to say to Jared? Oh hi Jared just been up to the Horton Tower to look at your latest handy work, oh by the way, why are you killing all these random folk of Wimborne, what delight have you got planned for doing me in?

The van came to a halt and, as he got out, the morning sun was way up and heating the front of the cottages. Jared's front door opened and Jared stood there in shorts and completely opened blue shirt. Matt looked over, a hairy chest and a smiling face greeted him. Matt saw red and anger took hold, the man was hiding secrets and he was a killer, he stormed up Jared's path and pushed him back into his own house,

Jared was caught off balance and stumbled backwards into his lounge, but army training kicked in along with some martial arts he'd learnt over the years, he swung his body round and centred his core, Matt came in pounding again, rage in his eyes, rage and upset. Jared had seen upset many times, his job was generally patching up soldiers if he could. He'd been posted to Afghanistan and numerous war torn areas in his time, some of the men never made it back. Yes, he had seen rage and upset before; he just didn't expect to see it being so eloquently displayed in his new neighbour. Jared was taking a pummelling so decided now was the time to take charge, sweeping his legs round completely took out Matt's footing and it was his turn to head for the lounge floor, only this time Jared sprang forward and slipping behind the falling Matt locked the man's arms as they both landed on the floor with Matt struggling on Jared's lap.

'Easy there Matt calm down buddy.' Jared locked Matt's arms but he was still struggling to free himself.'

'Let me go! You killed her didn't you? I've just been up to the tower.'

'Steady there, slow down. Killed who exactly?'

'Della! Della Dingles,'

'The post office owner?'

'Don't play ignorant with me,' Matt tried to struggle free as Jared had loosened his grip, but as soon as he moved, Jared's muscles tightened around his arms.

'Oh no you don't, you're going to listen to me. Why would I kill this Della Dingles?' Jared glared at the back of Matt's head thinking that he may try to head butt him so brought his chin forward and rested it on Matt's shoulder.

'W-what are you doing? Panic rose in Matt's voice.

'Safe guarding my good looks, come on answer me, why would I kill Della Dingles.' Jared could now feel all the tension running through Matt's body as he continued to struggle.

'Because her body was found with a piece of tree branch by it, I mean she was killed by having her neck slashed but a tree branch was nearby, it had blood, skin and some hair on it, the same colour as yours!'

'As I had nothing to do with it, it's hardly likely to be mine Matt is it?'

'Big coincidence though. You getting in late with a bloody big gash in your head.'

'I told you. Someone jumped me up at Perrins Wood, I needed to check on Miss Allmes.'

'So you say. Who is she to you?'

'Oh no, I'm still asking questions,' Jared commanded 'Why am I suddenly your murderer!' Jared finally lost his calm reserve.

'Della was with Arthur for a while – I don't know! Why did you kill Arthur? Was it jealousy? Their romance was over by the New Year, he chose you!'

Jared considered Matt's bile but was blown over by his last statement. 'What, Arthur and me?' he began to chuckle which annoyed the hell out of Matt who simply felt he couldn't really handle being a real detective anymore, besides he doubted he would live much longer.

'Are you going to kill me now?' was all that Matt could say, rather lamely too.

'Matt, I am a medic in the army, my goal in life is to mend people, put them back together, even those we consider as the enemy on some occasions. I don't kill them, I admit that I have not told you too much about things but that was only to protect you, your solicitor will explain everything, suffice to say, I do owe you an explanation but what I'm about to tell you will throw up more questions that I really want to leave to your visit to the solicitors, deal?'

Matt continued to wriggle to get free; Jared hung on, wrapping his legs around Matt's too.

'Just get on with it,' Matt said in disgust.

'It's difficult for me to say this out loud but, Arthur Jay is, was my father.'

Jared felt the tension leave Matt's body instantly and so, slowly loosened his hold on him but Matt leant back into his neighbour's arms and the two lay back exhausted.

Matt of course was thrown into deep confusion but simply said one thing. 'Sorry.'

Jared who was nestled on Matt's shoulder suddenly began to cry, for so long he had hidden his true identity and Matt was one of the few who knew it, but he was the only one that actually mattered when it came to the truth.

Matt turned and hugged his neighbour, 'Come on mate, is this the way for a soldier to behave?'

'You'd be surprised.' Came the tear choked reply

Matt watched Jared, his mind suddenly filled with excited confusion and a host of new ideas that he had never considered before.

Jared lifted his eyes and their eyes locked and the rest of the world suddenly didn't matter. Jared made the first move, lifting a hand to touch Matt's face.

Matt ever so slightly flinched as he too began to well up, some truths had lain hidden for so long, truths that he had never given grace to, the young man at the college must have somehow sensed the truth and built a fantasy up about it, a fantasy he had never encouraged, but now, sat before him was a man that excited him, a man that was instantly appealing to him but was he being duped and was he about to come out of a closet to a killer? Either way, the attraction was there. And it was mutual.

Jared broke his thoughts as he rose up and through their shared tears they began to kiss, gently at first, Jared tested his way, not wanting to upset Matt any more than he had done, but the connection completed both of them as a new found energy took control and suddenly they rolled together on the carpet kissing long and hard, feeling the strength and loving passion of kindred spirits.

George Blake studied the items that had been turned up at the Horton Tower murder scene, each encased in a plastic bag, three used condoms of different sizes and age, chewing gum, bicycle pump and an army knife, all found in the near surrounding area.

DCI Charles P Hepton swept into the office, 'What have you got for me George?'

'Well the condoms have an aged DNA range on it, suggesting that all three types have been around longer than the um, murder. The chewing gum didn't really measure anything but the army knife has a serial number on it that is unique to its owner, a Captain Jared Allmes, the thing is sir, well records show that he is actually Arthur Jay's son and lives, um sorry, lived next door to him at Horton Stoney, that and the fact that Della Dingles had had an affair with Jay…'

'George my sonner, I think we've got our man, come on, let's nab him.' Hepton said cheerfully his face alight with optimism.

Matt lay naked atop the white linen bed that belonged to Jared. He stared at the ceiling deep in thought but with a big smile across his face. Jared lay on his side propping his head up with his arm and watched Matt with mild amusement. 'What are you smiling about?'

For a moment Matt was quiet but then turned to look at Jared. 'Why me Jared?'

'Why you what?'

'Why did you, you know, kiss and things, oh, I'm not complaining.'

'I should think not, d'you know Matt, considering that we have only known each other for a few days I feel that I've known you for a long time. Arthur used to… sorry, I mean Dad used to tell me all about you, he said that I'd fall in love with you the moment I set eyes on you.'

Matt couldn't believe his ears, he didn't know where to start, fall in love? 'Arthur knew that you were um…'

Jared laughed, 'You can say it you know. Yes I'm gay Matt, everyone at work knows, thankfully I have never had a problem with it and yes Dad knew. He always told me that everyone deserved a chance in life, for years I could only see him on rare occasions, mum hated him having anything to do with us.'

'Us?'

'Ah, now here comes the things I don't really want to explain just yet, but by us I mean my brother.'

Matt nodded his head and smiled, he wasn't going to push Jared. Matt couldn't help but hope Jared was a good man, if the last few hours was anything to go by he had never in his life felt so special, so wanted by another person. How had he dropped his guard, how had Jared gotten in, a man!

'I can read you like a book Matt, you're in turmoil aren't you?' Jared still smiled that comforting smile that had warmed Matt from the moment he had first met him, which was in fact mere days ago, give or take each of them being knocked senseless.

'No, leave it out I'm fine.'

Jared raised a questioning eyebrow.

Matt gently laughed his eyes welling up. 'Look at this' he pointed at his tears. 'This isn't me, ok look, the thing we've done, I have never attempted, let alone wanted to do.'

'You think it a mistake?' Jared asked without sounding terse.

Matt sat up, eyes flooding again. 'That's just it. No, I have never connected with anyone like I have just done with you. Tell me, did your dad think that I was… gay?'

Jared gave a warm chuckle, ' He knew you were lost in the woods, he neither knew or cared what your preference was as long as you found your way, he mooted that there was a possibility of you playing for my team only because he could see you were so unhappy. I planned to meet you on this break home but, well things have got out of hand, the solicitor will put it all into perspective though Matt.'

'All this, the cottage and whatever the hell is waiting for me at Embridge, Embridge and Jones, it's all yours by rights, I can't accept any of it, it, it's wrong.'

'Now don't go thinking that stud, dad wanted you to have all this, I knew it, and what's more, whole heartedly agreed with it.'

'But why would you? I mean to say, why would your father who loved you so much not want to secure your future? Then there's your brother to take into account.'

'No! He will never be taken into account, he is a rogue, that's all you need to know for now.'

'Then tell me why, why me? There was silence before Matt added, 'please.'

Jared tipped his head sideways as he looked at Matt, his white teeth breaking into its usual smile. 'Suffice to say that our family are poison and you are the perfect tonic. You deserve it Matt and, I live next door to you, what could be better eh?'

Now, some time earlier when Matt had first arrived from the Horton Tower incident and crashed through the threshold of Jared's home, Mrs Doris Broadway watched the whole thing unfold from her cottage opposite. Now, she wasn't one to gossip but as the postman arrived with her mail she went to her front door, just to be sociable with Mr Prentice, a lovely warm spirited man in his forties who consistently wore shorts on his post rounds whatever the weather. It was as they happily talked that Doris noticed the bedroom curtains being drawn at Jared's home and casually dropped it into the conversation, two and two was added together and unlike in most cases where said sum made five, this time they were right on the money, assessing that there were now two gay gentlemen in residence at Stoney Horton.

The postman left Doris' home then drove back to Wimborne where he happened to mention the incident firstly to Bunty the Butcher who casually told Tim Bunn who was unfortunately the baker. Oh how he has laughed over the years when the general public drew his attention to the fact that he was Bunn the baker… this particular day, George Blake had popped in for six pasties and a cream horn for the team that were about to set off to arrest Jared Allmes, when Tim Bunn past on this latest piece of gossip which pretty much took George by surprise. Oh no, he thought. The governor is not going to like this, one jot.

'What! Matt Powers is a poof?' Hepton could hardly believe his ears 'I always knew he was lacking something but I never thought that he was a bum bandit.' He sniggered

George Blake just winced at the un-PC DCI, just too many initials to comprehend!

'Let's go and catch the buggers at it, I'd like to see the Police commissioner support him after this little act.' Hepton rushed out of his office cream horn in hand, Blake followed on lamely.

The latest bit of gossip which was truth, spread around Wimborne like a virulent plague within fifteen minutes, all in all, from the moment that Jared closed his bedroom curtains, to consummate a private and loving encounter with his neighbour, the word began to spread, until it was common knowledge thirty minutes later. At that point, two police cars screeched to a halt outside the cottage and four policemen, Hepton and Blake got out and ran up the path and began banging on the front door.

Now Doris who, as you may recall, was not one for gossip, watched the whole thing play out from her kitchen window and cursed the fact that she had no telephone to apprise people of the events unfolding.

Matt and Jared were already changed and back down in the lounge when the police arrived. Jared casually wandered to the door and was instantly man handled by two burly policemen backwards into the room. Hepton flounced in after them with that hawk like grin of self-importance. 'Well, well, well boys what have we been up to eh? The moment that my back's turned..., whoops. did I say my 'back's turned,' silly me, I meant that the moment one of you boys turned your back, the other one was... well I don't need to tell you the rest do I boys?'

Matt tutted and his eyes lifted to the ceiling in exasperation before locking onto Hepton. 'What in heaven's name has rattled your bush now?'

Hepton swelled with pride. 'Murder, you useless private dick, and your bitch here is our prime suspect, I think I could probably have you for aiding and abetting too, see how neatly I can have this all wrapped up.' Hepton began to strut.

Jared looked from Hepton to Matt, a worried look began to form. 'I'm innocent Matt, I promise.'

A policeman began to read Jared his rights while another man locked his hands in cuffs.

All the doubts returned to Matt but he tried not to show it. 'What's the evidence Hepton?' Matt suddenly shouted.

Hepton sneered. 'We have a knife with your serial number on Allmes.' Hepton stated over his shoulder to the incarcerated man while still sneering in Matt's direction. 'Well Powers, do I need to take you in as well or what?'

Matt was silent.

Jared tried to struggle between the two policemen. 'Matt, get to the solicitors, they'll fill you in on things.'

'Take him out men, I think we're done here don't you?'

Again Hepton strutted.

'Do you know Hepton, you're beginning to look like a friggin peacock, all that's missing is the feathers out of your arse!'

Hepton coughed with rage but decided to let it be, and marched out leaving Matt reflecting in the silent gloom. After what seemed an eternity he sprang up. 'To Embridge, Embridge and Jones then, I need answers and fast.' He spoke with a renewed urgency that suddenly ebbed away when he noticed a photo on the coffee table in Jared's lounge, surely he had put it there moments before the police had grabbed him, it was a photo of two identical women, twins but unless he was mistaken and he was sure that he wasn't, one of these women although taken many years ago had to be the reclusive and miserable old bat Miss Allmes.

6 SISTERS OF HATE

Beryl had handled the paperwork for the arrest of Jared Allmes. In the adjacent room was the evidence board, the only thing that tied him to the murders was the serial number of the knife that belonged to him as part of his army kit. Barry Berry was back on duty and dealing with the finger printing of said prisoner, he eyed Beryl, who was busy typing,

'You fancy her, do you?' Jared said with mild amusement.

'That's none of your damn business.' He spikily replied. 'Anyhow, what do you know about love? I hear you was caught with your pants down somewhere with a bloke when you was arrested.'

'And here I was thinking that you looked a nice guy, my mistake.'

'I'm sorry, I'm not used to being civil to cold blooded killers.' Barry was essentially a nice man, but being face to face with someone that was suspected of cold blooded murder brought out the finest bigot in him.

Barry took Jared's finger and placed it on an electronic scanner. Jared could tell that the policeman found it hard to face him. 'You do know that you should say alleged cold blooded killer, and as for being caught with my pants down, just remember not to believe everything you hear son, especially if it comes from that dinosaur Hepton. I think it not fair to drag your friend into this conversation, let him...' Jared stopped, suddenly realising that he was about to out Matt, maybe Barry wouldn't pursue it.

'My friend?'

Blast! There again, maybe Barry would, 'Ah, well I didn't mean to say anything and it's not right that I...'

'Just tell me, who the hell was you with?'

Beryl had just finished up typing the case notes, arching her eyebrows in surprise, at what Hepton had stated both Jared Allmes and one Matt Powers were doing prior to the arrest.

It was at this point that PC Barry Berry flew a punch at the prisoner, sending Jared backward while still sat at his seat, eventually sprawling to the floor, she ran up to Barry as Hepton and Blake came running out of a side office.

'Berry, what in heaven's name do you think you are doing?' Hepton shouted as Barry was held back by Beryl, blocking his way from any further onslaught.

Matt had entered the offices of Embridge, Embridge and Jones, just on the main square of Wimborne, above one of the Banks. The gold plated sign next to a plain door which led up some steps to a modern reception room where Georgina Bailey sat. The blonde bombshell looked up and smiled, Matt smiled back, and as he approached her he reflected that this was the woman that everyone in the town adored, and every man and even some woman wanted in their bed, well 'everyone' is an over statement, certainly there was a time when Matt may have considered her to, but alas, just maybe that ship has now sailed in the opposite direction.

'Hello Mr Powers, is it not?'

Wow, she even knew his name, and the way she said 'is it not' like some old arty film, 'Yes it is, what I mean is yes I am, hi.'

'Hello, again.' She smiled.

Oh Christ, she is going to think I'm flirting with her!' Matt panicked. 'Sorry, I'm a bit flustered, it's just, I was asked to pop round, no appointments necessary, I'm a bit over wrought with it all.' Nice recovery, she's not to know that it had suddenly become hard to talk to women after…, well, what he was doing with Jared last night, come to think of it, why was it difficult to talk to women now? maybe the failure of his marriage was because he was repressing Homosexual feelings… Homosexual, what a word, sounded like a sort of name a train might have – the Homosexual Express! Please leave your baggage at the door.

'Mr Powers?'

'Oh, sorry miss, I was day dreaming, is it possible to see Mr Embridge the younger, um Lance?'

Sleekly, Georgina's hands glided over to the telephone, her bangles rattling as she pressed the internal extension. 'Hello Mr Embridge, Mr Powers is here. He wondered if it would be convenient to see you now? Ok sir, I'll show him in.'

Georgina slid from her desk and headed toward one of the three doors that led off of reception. 'Follow me please Mr Powers, he'll see you right now.'

'Thank you.' Matt fell in step behind her as they entered.

'Here you are Mr Powers.' Lance stood up from behind an ornate desk, the room itself was incredibly large, with high windows that overlooked Wimborne square. Large blinds were slatted to filter out the brilliant sunshine that filled the room, a room with fine wood panelling and shelves of legal books.

'No please, everyone call me Matt.'

Georgina turned to him with that lovely smile 'Would you like a coffee or tea… Matt?'

'No thank you, I'm fine. Um perhaps some water, you know, normal tap stuff would be great, cheers.

Georgina left the room, the door closing silently behind her.

'What's this I've been hearing, you sly old fox.' Lance said changing his tune. 'And there was me thinking you didn't bat for the same team as me.'

'What, what' Matt felt panic lift in his stomach, 'What do you mean?'

'Come on now, this is Wimborne, you and Jared Allmes, I really am jealous; you're both so, gorrrr!'

Matt stood with his mouth open, looking like he was catching flies. He knew the folk of the town and it's propensity for local news, oh, why dress it up? Gossip. They loved gossip and it was an incredible network, but this mainframe of neighbourhood watch had truly excelled itself, maybe they had resorted to bugging everyones homes, oh God, was his new sexual experiences about to be broadcast on whatever the porn version of YouTube may be. Colour drained from his face and he slunk into one of the chairs facing the grand desk.

'Oh my dear man, what have I said?'

At that point Georgina returned with drinks and a file which she passed to Lance, she offered the glass of water to Matt who sat staring into space looking like a kicked puppy.

'Pop it on the Desk 'G', divert all my calls for now, thank you.' Lance said with a nod.

Georgina seductively retreated to the reception area once again shutting the door behind her.

'Now Matt, what's wrong? I'm a good listener, hey it's part of my job requirement.' Lance did his best to upbeat the conversation. 'I can do a song and dance number if you like?'

Matt suddenly realised the room around him and Lance's efforts broke him back into reality. 'So everybody knows about me and…?'

'Well I wouldn't say everybody.' Lance said trying to soften the impact

'Ok, given the efficiency of the town gossip network, how many would you guess, don't know that I slept with Jared?'

'Oh, so it really is true then?' Lance asked, his eyes wide in anticipation.

Shit, Matt thought, he had only just gone and verified the gossip. 'You are a solicitor right? So you must be bound by confidentiality…'

'At all cost.' Lance cut in, then made a zipping up mouth gesture.

'What's the point anyway, it came out of the blue, I've never done it before and the only time it happens…' Matt's conversation dried up.

Lance looked on and then gave one of his understanding smiles, with just a hint of his cosmetically whitened teeth.

Matt continued. 'Mr Embridge, I think I may have fallen for a killer.'

Lance was horrified, 'What, do you mean Jared Allmes? No, no, no, he is a good hard working man, his father was so proud of him.'

'Do you mean to say you knew that Arthur was Jared's father?' Matt stood up surprised and shocked.

Lance gestured for him to return to his seat. 'Please Matt, I think it best if I told you everything.'

'I wish someone would, Jared told me I should get the full story from you here as he didn't want to tell me himself.' Matt sat down slowly.

'That's because he is bound by the will not to say anything, there is a lot at stake, if it's any help, he was eager for you to know straight away but, well, we were still unsure.'

'About what exactly, all the way through this I have been kept in the dark, even Arthur has lied to me, be it his drinking or his circumstances, I must be a right asshole if the whole town knew his business and not me, ha Me, a detective.'

'No, now listen Matt, let me tell you everything.' Lance grabbed the file that Georgina brought in, he then sat down with it open in front of him, 'Yes, well first I need to tell you about Arthur's sisters...

Adeline and Leticia Allmes were twins; they were ten years older than Arthur and grew up in the county town of Dorchester. Adeline yearned to be an actress, floating around the rather large town house at the tender age of eleven, singing and dancing for whom ever would deem to listen. Leticia was more reserved and tended to sit in quiet corners with her head in a book. Mr Cornelius Allmes, their father had died during the war a year previous, leaving his wife Dora and the three children with an inheritance of three million pounds. Arthur was but a new born, so was completely oblivious. The girls were pretty switched on, although young, they easily grasped the concept of money, disappointing their mother by not even mourning their father or their dead sibling. The twins grew to be vile selfish girls, thinking nothing but of themselves. No man could show affection for such spiteful women. Dora Allmes, who had been constantly weak after the loss of her husband, was essentially a kind BUT meek woman, her broken heart affected her deeply, and to see how her twin daughters were growing without the guidance of a father figure made her suffer all the more. As Arthur grew, he understood more than he let on regards the pain his mum felt and when he was thirteen agreed to go and stay with his Uncle and Aunt, Barnaby and Maisy Jay in the village of Little Hodcum, just outside of Wimborne, while his mum recovered. Unfortunately he was never to return to his real home, his mum passed away leaving the house and entire fortune to Arthur. The house was to be sold and money from the sale to be divided between his sisters and his guardians, with the rest of the fortune to be his, once he came of age at twenty one. The sisters were furious and made numerous trips to Little Hodcum in a bid to overrule the Will and gain more of the monetary fortune that sat in the bank. Now, Barnaby and Maisy, although simple folk, were not stupid and knew full well what Adeline and Leticia were really like. Many times over the years Barnaby made mercy trips to Dorchester to sort out trouble that his nieces had caused his dear sister who's ailing health was as much to do with their behaviour as it was her broken heart.

The sisters didn't attend the funeral of their mother and, thanks to Barnaby, was told that they were no longer welcome in Little Hodcum. As time went on, one Christmas when Arthur was a teenager, he announced that he wanted to join the police service and so, once he was old enough, that's exactly what he did do.

Matt was once again shocked at the revelation that Old Arthur had been a Policeman once in his life. 'Are you telling me that Arthur, who was potentially a millionaire, became a Policeman Lance?'

'Well, basically yes, I suppose I am.' Lance said and then called Georgina for some more tea before he carried on with his story.

Over at the Police station it had become clear that there were no finger prints on the knife that tied Jared to the murder, but the blood on the branch did, eventually Reginald Embridge, the elder of Embridge, Embridge and Jones solicitors turned up and agreed bail allowing Jared to walk free, pending the police being able to form a case.

Reginald Embridge shook Jared's hand as they walked out of the police station.

'Thank you Mr Embridge, I don't know how you knew I was there but thank you.' Jared said, now showing visible relief.

Mr Reginald Embridge was a slight man, easily in his late fifties who, although outwardly a quiet man, had a voice of such strength that when he did speak everyone wanted to listen. He nodded in silent thoughts. 'Don't thank me, thank Georgina Bailey our secretary. Your' he paused not really sure how to put things, he wasn't a prude, just old fashioned in the dusty but lovable way, 'um friend is with my nephew now, finally finding out your legacy. She just happened to overhear that you had been taken by the police so, well I rushed down didn't I.'

'Why would you do that for me?'

'Because your father was essentially a good man Jared, he entrusted me, my company with the family estate of the Will and well, your wellbeing. He was a good judge of character my boy so if this Mr Powers is, well,' he paused again trying to find the right words that didn't sound patronising or, just plain wrong, 'important to you, I should add that Arthur thought of him like a son, well he would do if he has bequeathed the entice to him, what I mean is, I'm sure your dad would be proud if you two were…' Reginald nodded his head in self-agreement and pure joy, he liked how he had put things, shook Jared's hand once more then promptly walked off pleased with himself.

Jared smiled at the retreating dinosaur; he surmised that the man was genuinely kind but old fashioned. He thought for a moment, someone had jumped him while watching old Miss Allmes' house, and whoever it was had took the trouble to frame him for murder, the murder of the Post mistress. He decided to follow Mr Embridge's lead and head to the Solicitors; Matt was surely getting the whole potted history by now.

If Jared had looked up he would have noticed someone duck back behind an alley wall, someone who had watched and listened. As Jared walked off, the figure came out of hiding and headed in a different direction.

As Jared was about to cross the town square where the solicitors sat above the bank an old beat up Ford Escort with spoilers and go fast stripes pulled up and the horn sounded, Jared bent down to see who was beeping and his eyebrows rose in mild surprise.

'Oh, it's you.' He said in disgust.

The figure behind the steering wheel produced a gun with a nifty silencer on it.

'Would you really do it?' Jared asked.

Still the person remained silent and gestured with the gun for Jared to get in.

Jared looked around, there were people milling about but all were preoccupied. He glanced up to where the solicitors could be seen, almost willing Matt to look out one of the long stone framed sash windows, one last glance at the man he had loved the moment he set eyes on him. Jared was sure that getting into this car would be the death of him but, he had no choice.

Once Jared was in, the car sped off at break neck speed, tyres screeching at the off.

Matt was pacing the room trying to departmentalise these new bits of information, a sudden screeching of tyres from outside broke his thoughts and he casually looked out the window to see a clapped out Ford Escort wheel spinning away. 'Bloody boy racers.' He mumbled, then took a hearty gulp of fresh tea that the efficient and seductive Georgina had minced in and presented to them. Bloody hell, had he just thought the word minced into his memory. At this point, thoughts of Jared came flooding back into his mind. He realised that he believed Jared would not have killed his own father, not with all the genuine affection he had shown about him, no he couldn't believe it but, and this was a big but, he was sure that he knew something about who did. Why was he spying on his aunt's cottage? Miss Allmes couldn't have been killing people and why was Della a victim. His mind began to see patterns.

'Lance, which Miss Allmes is up at the cottage near Perrins Wood?' He looked over to the handsome solicitor who was sat at his desk watching Matt with curiosity.

'Oh that's easy, it's Leticia Allmes.'

'So where is Adeline?'

'Oh she left this country years and years ago, she lives in a gated community somewhere in California USA now.'

'Mmm still alive then.'

'You know what they say, only the good die young.'

'Do they?' was all Matt said absently. 'I think I need to hear the rest of this family story, and how exactly does it involve me?'

'Yes well, now we're refreshed let's begin.'

Arthur grew into a fine man, as far as I know he had little or no contact from his sisters until the day he was getting married to a lovely lady called Penelope Brown, she was the daughter of Fourdales Farm just to the west of Wimborne that was mixed Arable and Livestock, quite a big holding by all accounts. It was safe to say that they were well off and as Penelope was Minnie and Silas's only daughter, they were cautious but secretly over the moon that she had taken up with this newly qualified policeman with a rumoured fortune.

On the morning of the wedding, two bouquets arrived to the cottage you now own. These were the messages from his estranged sisters, both were bouquets of lilies and both had cards with obscenities written across it. It was clear that the sisters' hatred of their mother had been passed down to Arthur and it was all because of the inheritance, so Arthur washed his hands of them once and for all, sending each of them a damning letter telling them they would never be welcome in his or Penelope's life. As the years went on Penelope could still see the pain that his siblings had caused and one day, after coming out of the doctors high on the news that she and Arthur was expecting their first child, she attempted to contact the sisters via one address that Arthur kept in his drawer. It was to a house in Yeovil, she wrote of their wonderful news and how lovely it would be to have the whole family together. Nothing came back in reply. As the pregnancy progressed, they had some more cheerful and remarkable news, Penelope was expecting twins.

Again Matt interrupted the flow of Lance's tale, 'Arthur had twin sons, Jared is a twin?'

Lance replied awkwardly, 'Why, yes.' He shuffled in his seat, eager to continue.

Matt read the body language. 'Yes of course, well please continue, sorry.'

Lance smiled, sat back and continued.

Well once again the years went on, Penelope lost her parents and so Arthur and his sons Jared and Luke helped keep the farm going. The pressures began to show, Jared was determined to join the army and Luke tended to go out drinking a lot. Luke lived at the cottage while the rest of the family lived out at the farm, some say he was addicted to certain substances. It was around this time that he visited one of his Aunts, Leticia had moved back into the area and Luke would spend a lot of time with her. Arthur found out and indeed tried to offer an olive branch to her, only to be shunned at her front door with Luke sneering from behind Leticia in sheer spiteful delight.

The twin brothers grew distant as Jared began his army training, even more so when Jared learned that Luke was prosecuted for dealing in a particularly nasty drug and sent to prison with nothing but scorn for the rest of the family. Arthur and Penelope decided to sell the farm when his health took a dive and so moved back to the cottage. Just as things were getting better for them, with health improving and news that Jared had become a Doctor in the army and that the wayward Luke had finished his sentence and was due home, on a sunny autumn day as Penelope was walking back to Horton Stoney taking in the beauty of the countryside, a car which had been speeding, struck her full on, then proceeded on its way. The police never did find the culprit. Penelope had died instantly and Arthur was beyond consoling. This was the time that he really did drink. He started the Happiness Detective Agency with thoughts of bringing the hit and run culprit to book, but it was to no avail, the police said it was probably someone from out of the area, Arthur was a broken man.

Revelation after revelation filled Matt with despair, why had Arthur never shared this grief with him? Fundamentally Arthur was a lovely man, not once had he showed his real persona with Matt and this made him feel sad. 'I just wished he had told me something.'

'Oh don't feel bad, he trusted you completely, you are inheriting his fortune.'

'But why Lance?' Matt stood again 'Why do I inherit and not his sons?'

'He knew money would destroy his family, the sisters were flying around again, both Leticia and Adeline was sending vile mail to him, they even paid for a stripper to turn up at Penelope's wake. Luke tended to hang around Leticia's cottage, the rumour mill worked over time suggesting that they had a little criminal business running there. Jared came and stayed with his father for a while, that's when the cottage next door became available and Jared bought it with his own earnings and mortgage, it was a gesture that opened Arthur's heart again. He realised that Jared was a sorted, responsible adult with no eye on the inheritance. Arthur stopped drinking and began living again, he maintained this image though, because he didn't trust his sisters and so thought if he looked incapacitated, then he would be deemed no threat just a drunken waster. It worked as an advantage in his detective work also; he did like to smoke though.

Lance reshuffled some of his notes. 'Are you keeping up with this?'

Matt laughed, 'Like a bloody soap opera man. I still don't know why I get the inheritance.'

'I'll be getting to that.'

More years passed, a sort of truce fell between Arthur and Leticia, only Mr Embridge senior knew of the true facts regarding Arthur and his siblings, the rest of the town even to this day think that he had no family. The folk at Horton Stoney don't recall the family as such although they knew he lost his wife but time has made Arthur Allmes Jay's true history vague, even for the most resolute gossipers, the sons were never connected to him because they had their true surname where as he remained Mr Jay. He vowed to do something good with the fortune, a considerable percentage would be paid monthly to his sisters and his sons but a clause was written in the agreement and the Will stating, that no family member would be able to influence anyone connected to the inheritance or they will forfeit their entitlement and that on passing, there will be enough put by to continue their monthly entitlement for thirty years. The rest would be paid to whomever Arthur A Jays named as benefactor.

'And that's me?'

'Most certainly is.'

'So I inherit whatever is left from his three million fortune. I really can't believe this. How much do the family get a month then?'

Lance flustered before answering, 'Well they are all set up well, each receiving four thousand pounds a month, Jared certainly has no need to work but he does. He feels he needs to make a difference, his Dad was so proud of him.'

'And Luke, what sort of mess is he making of his life?'

'We don't know, he lives in London somewhere, has nothing to do with the family. He fell out with his Aunt years ago, not sure about Adeline in America, but as you see, not the most harmonious of families.'

'Ok, tell me, there can't be much of this inheritance left for me then, I have to admit, I'm somewhat relieved that this three million isn't coming my way, apart from Jared, this family strikes me as dangerous and with that amount hanging over my head, I'd hate to think what…' What in hell had he just said, was there the slightest chance that Arthur was killed because of the Will, surely not?

Lance stood and then walked over to Matt, 'Where are you plucking this three million idea from, you're not getting that.'

'I should think not, the cottage is more than I could ever have wished for, good old Arty.'

'Twenty eight Million,' Lance simply stated folding his arms, quietly watching Matt's face as he stood before him.

'Twenty eight million what Lance?' Matt screwed his face slightly, confused at what Lance was alluding to.

'The money that is now rightly yours is twenty eight and a quarter million pounds. The farm land was sitting on a vein of oil when he sold it. You could argue that this fortune belongs to Penelope's family. Well, as a couple they did inherit the farm land and she has no other family, but Arthur's family found out somehow. The weeks leading up to Arthurs murder, I think we received twelve appeals from his sisters and son Luke requesting the right for a larger share of the fortune, when that didn't work, we started receiving the usual hate mail, must be a speciality of the sisters, I call them arsenic and old lace.'

'Twenty eight million pounds… oh Fu…!'

7 DANGEROUS RELATIONS

Beryl took Barry for a pint at the Crown. He clearly had issues that needed resolving and as she had finally found her voice and knew who she was, she suddenly felt empowered to help her colleague and her friend. 'Why did you react like that earlier Barry, Hepton is like a bear with a sore head, the last thing you want to do is piss him off.'

'I don't want to talk about it.' Barry snapped.

'Well, clearly you do or you wouldn't have come to the pub with me.' Beryl kept calm, retaining that quietness that she instilled.

Barry took a long sip of his lager that Beryl had presented to him. He glanced around the busy late afternoon bar room. Bess or Darren were nowhere to be seen and a couple of young barmen and a barwoman busied themselves with the punters. From the corner of the room he quietly took in the hustle and bustle and then finally spoke.

'Why is the whole world turning gay?'

'What?'

'Well, there is you and the butcher woman…'

'Bunty, her name is Bunty.' Beryl spiked slightly, a verbal reflex warning.

Barry looked forlorn, 'I really liked you.'

'Well unless I've died or eloped to Skegness…'

'I mean, really liked you…'

'Oh, I see. Look Barry, you have that mouse from the office now, she's kind of nice. I love Bunty, and I'm not going to change the way I feel, but this whole conversation isn't about us is it? I wager that you are reacting to the fact that a friend of yours has just been outed by the town gossips and you can't handle it.' Beryl's eyes glared at him bear like.

'I've known Matt for years Beryl, he never told me. He was married for God sake!' Barry conceded.

Beryl laughed 'You stupid man, you're more upset that he never told you.'

'Yes I am, we're supposed to be mates, we're not meant to have secrets.'

'You're not that close to him, when was the last time you went out with him?'

'We went to a rugby match, The Wimborne Martyrs versus The Dorchester Warriors in November, and I didn't 'go out with him' as you put it, we hung out!'

'Ooh really?' Beryl teased.

'You know what I mean!'

'Barry Berry, you are homophobic!'

'Eh, I am not, I like the sport only, well we know it wasn't just the match that Matt must have been watching!'

Beryl stood up angrily, 'Well I for one am not staying to listen to this bile. I'd say Matt is lucky to lose you as a friend, right when he needs you too, you should be ashamed.'

'Beryl wait! Barry's eyebrows creased upward in the middle. Beryl eyed him with rage but he still held his pitiful gaze.

'Ok, I'm a sodding idiot; I was shocked and bloody useless to run to his defence. Is that what you want to hear?'

'It'll do for starters.' Beryl smiled, and sat back down. 'It's not me you should be talking to anyway.'

'Well given the chance, I promise I'll make it up with him.' A smile almost broke on his face.

'It's your lucky day, look who's just walked in.' Beryl waved.

Matt was in shock and decided to leave the comfort of Embridge, Embridge and Jones and head for the sanctuary of the Crown and Bess with her ample bosom. He was out of luck, Bess wasn't there, not that he was into breast anymore, was he ever into womens' breasts, probably not, if he was honest. At this point of reflection, the waving hand of Beryl caught his eye and he smiled and headed over. Barry was sat not turning, mmm not good, Matt thought as he sat down beside him,

'Alright Matt…' Barry was polite and made the most sparing conversation but refused to look Matt in the eye.

Beryl looked on pityingly

Matt was no fool. 'I see the town intra net in all things gossip has reached you then buddy.'

Barry finally looked up at Matt. 'What have you been doing today then?'

Beryl watched silently, yes, Barry was trying.

And then he ruined it… 'Oh God, when I said, what have you been doing? I didn't mean who have you been do…, well you know, sort of man on man action stuff, I'm not interested in that, oh God, what I mean to say is that I'm not remotely interested in men, not in that way, I was just…'

'Barry you bloody Burk. I am not suddenly shagging the entire male population of Wimborne, don't you know. I know you're not gay, and never once thought you were. Bloody hell, I didn't even know that I…till, well recently, besides I don't fancy you.'

'What about going to watch the rugby eh?'

'What about the rugby? Oh I see, well I must confess to not really liking rugby but I went, just to hang around with a friend, you, you bloody fool, my plutonic good natured buddy.'

'I'll get some more drinks.' Beryl added as she shot to the bar smiling.

Barry relaxed, then looked at Matt, asking earnestly. 'So what's so wrong, that you don't fancy me then…'

Matt laughed.

Mick Dingles had been drugged. Hours before he had answered the door of his large extended house to find someone standing there that scared him. The person stepped into his home and while Mick comprehended who it was standing before him; he found a hypodermic needle pressed sleekly into his neck and then unconsciousness washed over him.

He eventually woke to find himself gagged and strapped to his four poster bed with the instant smell of petrol fumes around him, he wasn't sure if it was the remnants of the drug that was pressed into his system earlier or the fumes from the fuel that made his head swim, unfortunately he was never to find out. The phantom intruder entered the bedroom and despite the muffled objections from Mick, made no attempt to communicate. He rummaged in the pockets of his hooded duffle coat before producing a lighter, he flipped the lid which in turn produced a flame and then threw it at the bed.

The duffle coated killer retreated quickly as the room became a torrent of angry flames. Mick's gagged screams were barely audible in the rage of the searing heat and fire and soon ebbed into oblivion, where his wife no doubt waited with an angel and a devil on her arm.

Matt, Beryl and Barry were still in the Pub when fire engines could be heard in the distance, Barry and Beryl were in shock, and so chose to ignore the sound, Matt had just informed them of his inheritance.

'That is just an obscene amount of money Matt, what are you going to do?'

'Well given half the chance I'd want to give it back to the family.'

'But you can't, by all accounts the family is rotten.' Beryl cut in, 'Excluding Jared, of course.'

'Arthur put a clause in, just for me, 'If I was to give substantial amounts back to his family without it directly benefiting said nominee, that's me, then the entire amount would be forfeit and would be given away to the only place that he knew that would really annoy me.'

'Who to? Barry asked.

'The Tory party, the old goat has stitched me up good and proper.'

Both Barry and Beryl burst out laughing, it was laughter that didn't seem to subside. At first Matt looked hopping mad, but after a short while couldn't help but join in, all three becoming hysterical. Eventually they regained their dignity.

'So Jared is a free man?' Matt asked

'Well only until Hepton can build a case against him.' Barry said

'I need to start pulling some of these threads together. Jared's innocent, that I'm sure but I have a hunch, and it's all to do with those twins. Beryl do you think you could find out everything you can about the family? Concentrate on Arthur and Penelope Jay, I've an inkling that Della Dingles has been blackmailing Arthur, I'm beginning to think that whole affair that he had with her was a complete and utter set up.

'Bloody hell Matt, old Hepton hasn't pulled those ideas together yet.' Barry laughed.

'I'm going home now, that's if I still have a home to go too, living in Horton Stoney, the neighbours might burn gay people.' Matt said.

'Matt, be careful,' Barry warned, ' There is definitely a killer out there, and it's likely that this fortune, inheritance, whatever you want to call it is the catalyst, now that it's officially yours, well it makes you the target doesn't it?'

'With a last glance at his friends he raised an eyebrow. 'Don't you hold back will you Baz, see you tomorrow.' Matt turned and walked out the door.

Barry and Beryl sat watching him leave, 'Maybe we should inform Hepton.' Beryl said.

'Whatever for, they rub each other up the wrong way.'

'But Matt really is in danger, we need to let Hepton hear the theories, if he chooses to ignore them, well, we can cross that bridge when we come to it.'

Barry grabbed Beryl's hand. 'You're right again, of course. Beryl, thank you for looking out for me, for giving me the time, you know?

'Yes' she said cheerfully, 'yes I know.'

'Oi, put my girlfriend down!' came a booming voice. Bunty cut her way through the throng heading for the two off duty police officers.

Barry looked from Bunty to Beryl and then did something quite easily that he never thought possible, he smiled.

It was a curious thing, as Matt came out of the Crown, he noticed across the road, in the dimming evening light of the threatening cloudy skies, the witch like qualities of the wretched Miss Allmes, who had appeared to notice him before getting into a battered ford escort, shoeing the black poodle onto the back seat, now was his chance to go and ask her about her brother, maybe she'll come clean, now that he knew some truth. Matt broke into a jog to approach the car, suddenly he heard a voice, a familiar voice, but not one he could place, shouting angrily to the old harridan, she cursed the male driver but finally sunk into the front seat slamming the door shut, the vehicle then screeched off before Matt could get to it. The car sped past Matt, with the cold emotionless eyes of Leticia Allmes firmly trained on him, the driver had a big hood up, it was almost as if he didn't want Matt to see his face, then he remembered the car from earlier. 'The boy racer' He said.

It was just beginning to rain heavy as Matt pulled his faithful yellow and white VW Campervan into Horton Stoney, pulling up outside 18 Grange View, his home. Hail as well as rain battered against the roof of the van so Matt didn't hang about getting from van to cottage, taking in the fact that a light was on in Jared's lounge but he resisted the notion of stopping there first. No, he needed to have a bath, a nice long bath and reflect on the latest bits of information along with the fact that he actually didn't have to work anymore.

Within fifteen minutes Matt was sinking into a mass of bubbles that topped a nice hot bath, a glass of rosé and a hot buttered muffin sat on the closed toilet seat, to the side. 'Bliss,' He said to himself as he allowed the bubbles and water to overwhelm him as he sunk under its depths. After several submersions, Matt could make out the muffled drone of the doorbell; he surfaced, spitting water out from his mouth and nose. Grabbing a towel, he stepped out hurriedly and grabbed a robe before heading bare footed for the door.

Half expecting to see Jared standing there, Matt was surprised to see the dripping wet form of old Mr…What's his name, same as his dogs, that's it! 'Hello Wilf, rough night to be out, come in, you'll catch your death.'

'I shan't boy, just checking you're alright.'

'Of course, look it's very nice to see you but as you see.' Matt gestured his bathrobe attire.

Wilf grunted then carried on regardless. 'We have some mentionings rumbling around that might be of use to you.'

Matt sighed, 'Gossip you mean.'

'Don't be so dismissive young'un. Aye, gossip it maybe, but in these ere parts gossip isn't just hearsay.

Matt couldn't help but like the abrasive old country geezer. 'Will you step in or what, you may have the constitution of one of those grass chewing bovines but I don't.'

'You townies are all the same.' Wilf mumbled as he finally stepped into Matt's cottage.

Next door, Jared silently closed, his slightly ajar front door, unable to hear his neighbour's continuing conversation.

'Arthur was being blackmailed.' Wilf stated from the sofa as Matt had re-emerged, with hot cocoa.

'I had kind of taken a leap of faith on that one. Do you know who and why?'

'The Dingles woman. The silly fool had told her everything during their courtship.'

Courtship, blimey, Matt hadn't heard those terms for many years. 'Mmmm a married woman too.'

'Della Dingles wasn't married to that big buffoon, they lived in sin didn't they! No, they knew what they were doing, found out he was worth a mint through personal mail didn't she, that's when she took an interest, eventually her so called husband was roped in. Poor old bugger was heartbroken wasn't he. He did confide bits to me but I ain't spoken to anyone about it, at least, not until now.'

'What are you telling me Wilf?' Matt sat opposite him, eager to listen.

'She was going to marry Arthur you know?'

Matt shook his head numbly.

'The word is they would have married to get the fortune but Arthur found out, broke off the plans. That's when she and her partner blackmailed him, saying the facts of his real identity and his broken family would be given over for gossip.

'Why would Arthur worry what people thought?'

'Because he didn't want to be associated with them, his family is poison. He loved his sons but even one of those let him down. The boy next door was his pride and joy, gave him hope. He always hoped you would both be, well whatever you call a pair of wedded bum boys.' Wilf talked on, the connotation that this was a derogatory comment was ridiculous, and Wilf spouted it as simple un-demeaning fact.

'Arty knew I was gay before I did.'

'Aye lad, he was a wise one. Matt, you and Jared would make him so happy, he'd be jumping on his cloud.

Matt was stunned, Wilf had just referred to him and his neighbour by their Christian names.

'So, is it down to pride that Arthur didn't want the truth spelled out.'

'Pride can be destructive boy, but so can gossip, once it has been twisted out of shape.'

'I see.' Matt said, not really understanding, but there again, he wouldn't want his own divorce business to be spread all around the town.

Soon Wilf was on his way into the night, wearing one of Matt's spare woollen hats with built in ear coverings.

He sat silently for a while, so the Dingles had bitten off more than they could chew. Had Arthur arranged to kill her from his grave? Ridiculous, Arthur wasn't like that, but as had been demonstrated so well in the past few weeks, what did he really know about Arthur anyway? He got up looking at the clock. It was eleven fifteen, time for bed. The doorbell rang again. He opened the door to find Jared standing naked, wearing nothing but a smile.

'Are you crazy?' Matt dragged him in, hoping nobody in the hamlet had noticed.

Jared was surprisingly quiet, but quickly worked on removing Matt's bathrobe before he could object. The heavy petting on the lounge floor gave way to Jared grabbing the belt of the discarded bathrobe and tying the hands of Matt, who began to object.

As much as he tried Matt couldn't stop Jared, the stronger he fought, the happier the silent Jared appeared to be. Matt, hands now tied firmly behind his back made to stand up.

Jared finally spoke, 'Oh no you don't lover, you're mine now!'

With that, Jared chopped sharply at the back of Matt's neck, causing him to collapse back down onto the floor dazed, through the mist of confusion he could clearly see how excited that this made Jared and felt the pain as his body was about to be invaded without consent, but then, at the point of almost unconsciousness Matt pulled back, finding strength, he twisted sending Jared flying, but Jared rolled over once and was on his feet and pinning Matt up against the wall before he could turn to run.

'No you don't, we belong together now, you and me against the world.'

'What's happened to you?' Matt turned his face away as Jared tried to kiss him.'

'Don't look away from me.' Jared warned.

'Leave!' Matt said as loud as he could.

Jared stared at him for a few moments, still excited, almost animalistic, nothing like his gentle loving self from the previous night. He drew close to Matt's ear and growled like a dog before gently nibbling his ear.

Despite the horrific situation, Matt's body reacted favourably to this new approach. Jared suddenly licked the side of his face in one long stroke that made it instantly obvious to Jared how pleasurable this was but as Jared coursed his tongue down across Matt's chest and down over the ridges of his six-pack, a knee came up and blasted Jared in the face. The effect was instant; Jared was out cold, a bloody nose for his trouble. Matt panicked, maybe he had killed him. He awkwardly kneeled down and could make out the steady rise and fall of his torso. The next thing was for him to free his hands, which happened easily away from the blind panic of someone trying to rape him. Why had he done this to Matt? What the hell was going on, there was no way he could report him, not after losing his father like this but, was Jared the killer after all. It was while looking away for a moment that he heard Jared's calm voice.

'I'm sorry.'

Matt spun round. Jared was perched up on his elbows, blood and tears across his face. 'You're sorry!' Matt started to laugh, a soulless hollow laugh. 'I trusted you, your father trusted you, we... Last night, you turned my world around, tonight you have destroyed it.'

'I want you to know it isn't personal, it's me.'

Matt did not understand or want to understand, at this point he noticed Jared was recovering down below, things were beginning to stir so quickly. Matt removed his own bathrobe once more and threw it at Jared who was watching with that animal glint in his eyes again. 'Just go Jared.'

Jared got up, grasping the bathrobe but parading his muscular physique in front of Matt one last time. Matt turned away in disgust, more because he could feel those twinges of excitement deep within himself. Jared could see, and stared at Matt's fine naked back and buttocks. Matt felt the eyes burning into him. 'I said go! In future, don't talk to me or come near me even. If you do, then I'll call the police.'

Jared tilted his head in thought, smiled then left, without the bathrobe, making sure that his nakedness brushed against Matt as he went out the door.

Matt heard the front door close and breathed a sigh of relief. After putting on his bathrobe and sitting quietly he suddenly jumped up and ran up to his bedroom, finding his mobile phone he called Barry. It was two in the morning.

Barry stirred in his double bed as his mobile sprang into life. Suddenly he was wide awake, often his station would call for him to come into work at awkward hours, so he was used to switching to alert mode, he was surprised therefore to see Matt Powers name light up.

'Matt, are you ok, what's happened?'

'Barry, I think the other twin is next door to my cottage.'

'What do you mean? What twin, do you mean the Allmes sister? What's she doing there?'

'No, listen to me!' Matt was on edge.

'Ok, I'm listening.' Barry conceded.

'I think that Jared Allmes twin brother is next door, the thing is, I don't know what has happened to Jared himself, I think he may be in danger, or worse.' Matt winced in pain as bruising was starting come out all over his body.

'Jared has a twin?' Barry said, not wanting a reply.

'Get cars over here Barry, I'm telling you.' Matt hung up, then quickly got changed. Turning off the light he parted the curtains, just then a car approached and pulled up by his van, the rain was now mizzle in the night sky so it was practically impossible to see who it was, just then light spilled from next door as the front door was opened, then he could just make out Jared running toward the car, Matt pulled open the window to get a better look and made out the car, it was the ford escort, a figure got out.

'You useless idiot get in!' The figure said, again he was hooded. The figure spotted him and pointed, Jared turned from the open passenger door to look as something ricocheted off the wall near where Matt was watching.

Bloody hell, he was shooting at him. Matt stayed ducked down, as he once again heard the escort eventually screech away at speed. Matt kept mulling over the words that the hooded figure had shouted – 'You useless idiot get in.' the voice was so familiar, but who was it. Matt remembered Wilf's assessment – 'His family is poison...' that's what Wilf had said, except, that was what he relayed from Arthur's opinion, Arthur Jay had thought his family poison, blimey, his family tree was a gathering of dangerous relations, no wonder he never talked about them... Talk, TALK! At this point Matt knew where he had heard the mystery driver's voice from, it was Arthur Jay!

8 MAKE A WISH

How could he have not recognised the old man's voice, but how in the name of God did he cheat death, and to what ends? This was yet another situation that didn't add up. The lights flashing outside signalled the arrival of the police cars, although there were no sirens, the whole hamlet was bathed in a flashing blue dawn, and those curtain twitchers will be sharpening their pencils for the early morning addition of gossip no doubt.

There was a bang on the door and Matt was relieved to find Beryl and Barry standing there, neither in uniform but there were at least four other appropriately dressed officers running next door, just then his stomach sank as in the distant mizzle, he saw the distinctive form of DCI Hepton.

Barry checked over his shoulder. 'It's ok Matt, he's not as bad as he seems. He'll listen to you.'

'Hey, Ass bandit, what happened, a lover's tiff?' Came the all too familiar boom of Hepton.

Matt glared at Barry. 'Are you perfectly sure of that Bazzer?'

They were sat in Matt's lounge drinking coffee. Matt was sat next to Beryl on the sofa, opposite Hepton sat studying them as Barry came in. 'Next door is clear sir.'

'Good boy, now bugger off and leave it to those that are suitably attired.' Hepton looked Matt up and down, and then his eyes fell on Beryl. 'That goes for you too Tinker Bell.'

Beryl left the room with a glare at Hepton followed by a soothing look toward Matt.

'That girl's getting there.' Hepton said

Matt just shook his head in dismay.

'Oh, you think I'm just a misogynistic mouthpiece with no thoughts for others?'

'No, those words didn't spring to mind I must admit but as we're going there, I do find you utterly repellent, oh and you can add homophobe to the list as well as ex-DCI if I chose to report all your inappropriate comments and behaviour.' Matt spat.

'And here's me thinking that we had something…'

'What?' Oh God, not you too. Matt thought to himself.

Hepton must have read the thoughts all over Matt's panic stricken face. 'No, no, no, no, I don't mean I'm one of your lot Powers. Look I admit that at first, you irritated the hell out of me, all I could see was a suspect getting away with it and even if you were innocent, you'd have grand ideas of being some private hero and interfere in Police business. Well, if I'm honest I still do but, and this is a big but, now that Mick Dingles has been confirmed as murdered…'

'Mick Dingles, how, when?'

'Found burnt to death in his home yesterday evening, while you were with those two clowns of mine. Listen Powers, Matt, Someone is killing people on my turf and I don't like that. What is more, from what Berry and the munchkin has told me, all of it is to do with your inheritance…'

'They told you?' Matt blasted.

'Oh don't get all precious on me sweetheart.' Hepton replied in his usual pig-headed way.

'And there you go again, you just can't help yourself can you? What is it with you and these stupid comments, do you find gay people a threat because, believe me, I'm having a little trouble getting my head around things myself at the moment. What do you want me to do? Shall I go put my head in the oven or something eh? Eh!' Matt demanded, going red in the face and veins protruding from his neck.

Hepton looked nonplussed throughout the verbal onslaught. Strange, thought Matt, considering how Hepton used to react to Matt being around, but then the DCI turned to him with the kindest of expressions, brought his hand up to Matt's face and slapped his cheek a couple of times.

'My son was gay.' Hepton said then walked to the curtain and peered out.

Matt calmed, 'What do you mean, was?'

'He died,'

Had Hepton's voice just faltered?

Hepton turned, knowing that he had just revealed something he could never take back, and to Matt's astonishment he could plainly see merest pearls of tears in the man's eyes.

Matt didn't know what to say and was somewhat taken aback. When Hepton finally sat next to him, gone was the aggressive monster. Before him was a glimpse of a broken man who got through the day raging at the world.

'Now you know.' Hepton said

'I'm so sorry.' Matt offered, not sure if it was the right thing to say.

'DCI Charles P Hepton, divorcee, bully and all out bastard, my boy was being bullied and I was too busy to notice. He was twenty one and…' Hepton's voice broke and Matt lifted a cautious hand up and placed it on his shoulder. 'I was at the New Year Ball with Wendy, my wife, ex-wife, five years ago now. As far as we knew, our son Pete was out celebrating with friends except,' Hepton paused again, finding it increasingly hard to express, Matt even resulted to rubbing his back but felt less awkward. Before him was a fellow human being in distress, 'Of all the times to break down.' Hepton added.

'Why have you been such a bastard to me?' Matt asked, yes he wanted to know what had happened to Pete Hepton but there was still a spike in his gut that distrusted the DCI and his bigotry.

Hepton huffed an empty laugh. 'The moment I saw you, reminded me of my boy, I even reckoned you were gay, oh I know you didn't know it, but I could see the traits.'

'Thanks a lot, I'm underwhelmed.' Matt objected.

Hepton looked at Matt, eyes now dry. Hepton's brown eyes bore into him for what seemed ages before he spoke again. 'He hung himself, while we were out enjoying ourselves, he went into the garage and using some washing line cord tied to the roofing beams he stepped from a chair and…' The eyes continued to freeze Matt, like a rabbit in headlights. 'My wife left me soon after, saying I was unbearable, she took up with some jewellery shop owner and now has another child. Me, well as you said, I'm just a homophobic and misogynistic mouthpiece that probably died out with the dinosaurs.'

'But I didn't know the facts did I?' Matt hated how the whole conversation had turned.

'Believe me, I had no intentions of telling you, I mean to say, of all people!'

'Shut up Hepton, we need to sort this current problem out,' Matt felt daring enough to challenge him, 'Then you need to take stock, but not alone, I'll help.'

'You, do you think this little heart to heart, constitutes friendship?' Hepton tried to regain his hard crusted shell.

'Well, if you were honest Detective Chief Inspector, yes, against all odds, you and I are friends. The sooner you come to terms with this little twist in the scenario the better, so stop being such an ass hole.' Matt stood looking, determined not to be brow beaten again.'

Hepton stood staring, his eyes wide in, was it rage? But then, the corners of his mouth turned up into a smile and he stepped forward and gave Matt, what felt like a fatherly hug.

'Ok Matt, tell me what you know, let's go catch us a killer.

The Police arrived on mass at the cottage of Miss Allmes; Matt was allowed to travel with the DCI, which confused the hell out of his officers. Barry and Beryl had gone onto the station, getting into uniform on the way.

Matt counted ten officers spreading out around the cottage, which sat silent and dark. The police had strong torches to light the area up. The clouds covered the sky making it pitch black. 'There's no car.' Matt stated.

Hepton, who strolled ahead of him looked over his shoulder, 'What do you mean?'

'The Ford Escort, it's not here.'

'Mmm, by now they may have thought to ditch it.'

'And would have expected me to connect this place with them?'

'Still have to check it though Matt, Who knows maybe we'll find Jared.'

Matt didn't share the fear that he felt inside, that just maybe, Jared was Luke all along, the convenient neighbour, but surely the idea would have been to get on his good side, romance him even, just to get hold of the blasted fortune. Inwardly he winced, convinced he had just been used, what was worse was he had been outed all for nothing but a false premise. Then he noticed Hepton walking ahead of him and thought that his own emotional problems were nothing to the pain that man was concealing.

They hammered on the front door, not a sound could be heard.

'Maybe they sleep heavy.' Hepton suggested.

'The dog,' Matt said

'What dog?' Hepton snapped.

'The Allmes sisters had a black poodle. The last time I was here it barked constantly but, well there's no barking.'

'Harris, Preston, if you would please.' Hepton asked of the two officers behind them. They stepped forward; one policeman was holding a tubular piece of metal which, once he stepped ahead of them, he swung back and rammed the front door. The door gave way instantly, flying open without protest. The hall way was pitch black but one of the officers soon found a light switch which bathed the hallway and the front area of the cottage garden in light. The sight before them caused Matt to step back, only to tread on the toes of another officer coming through the threshold of the front door.

Miss Allmes lay on the floor, her thin loose neck clearly broken, atop her fallen body was the remains of a poodle which had been filleted and deliberately placed with entrails spread across her body.

'Sick bastards.' Matt said.

'Spread out, this is a murder scene, someone call for back up, I want this place searched, leave no speck of dust unturned, Hepton demanded, then added, 'With gloves!'

Hepton was pretty busy from then on. Matt had a look about the untidy, unkempt home, finally stepping out the back door staring at the dark garden and the old well at the end of the boundary where the land ran up to Preston Wood. Several people had definitely been staying in the cottage, no sign of the other sister though, maybe she was never there. He began to think of Jared/Luke, deep down he had hoped that Jared did exist and they would find him bound gagged and perfectly ok but, nothing. The funny thing was that, because there was no sign of a Jared body, it kind of confirmed to Matt his darkest fears; he had been seeing Luke right from the very beginning.

'You ok?' Matt turned to find Hepton standing at the back door.

'How did Arthur do it, how did he cheat death and fool everyone?'

'Well, I've got your two little friends onto it, Beryl is looking into the family connections, now that we know his true family tree and Barry is checking the Autopsy report and, well we may have to exhume his body.'

'Who the hell did they bury?' Matt asked, not expecting an answer.

'That's the whole point Matt. We need to give whoever it is a proper burial. Who knows, maybe old Arthur had a double. You get off home now Powers, leave this work to us, those responsible are long gone I'm sure; they obviously know we're on to them. If anything turns up, we'll let you know straight away, hey I'll even throw in a constable to watch over you while you sleep, he won't be tucking you in though.' Hepton said with a glint in his eye.

'Sure, can I get a lift home? It's a long walk across country and I didn't bring a bike.' As he said bike his eyes fixed on a bike leant against the old coal house. 'That was Art's, he was riding it here the night he… except he didn't die did he?' Something dawned on Matt, an awakening of such magnitude, something that rung bells when he heard about it earlier. 'I need to see Beryl DCI, I have a hunch.'

'Leave the hunches to us, these are deadly people we are dealing with…'

'But…'

'No, go home Powers or you and me are back to square one! We'll catch up with your two friends in the morning, together!' Hepton spoke with determination, once again that edgy warning tone had returned that he used to often put people down, but he still retained the new likable angle that had surfaced in his front lounge earlier.

PC Baines took one of the squad cars and was ordered to take Matt home and stay, overlooking the Private Detective's safety. Baines liked westerns and as he drove into Horton Stoney he imagined he was the sheriff of a small gun toting town, well he had a vivid imagination and considering the silence coming from Matt, he had nothing else to think of.

The little Hamlet was quiet again. Matt was no fool though, he was sure that beady eyes were scanning them as they arrived even though it was five am and gone, he expected that many of them were up early anyway.

PC Baines followed Matt up to the front door and followed him in.

'Would you like a cuppa Constable?'

'I'd love one sir thank you.'

'None of that buddy, call me Matt.'

'…And you can call me…' The words stuck in Baines throat as he walked through to the lounge to find an old man holding a gun to Matt's head.

Arthur Jay stood there, alive and well, his eyes looked just mad enough to shoot Matt's brains out. 'Now isn't that touching? Do you fancy the private Dick too then Constable?'

'No sir, now let's not be hasty here, no one is armed…'

'Apart from me.'

'Yes well, apart from you.'

'Easy Baines, this monster is dangerous enough to shoot.'

At that point, from behind the open lounge door stepped Luke Allmes with a hypodermic in hand.

Arthur's hand slipped over the protesting Matt, it was too late for Baines, as the needle was pressed into the Policeman's neck and his reaction was almost immediately numbed as he collapsed. Luke managed to catch the man and gently eased him onto the floor; he took the cap off the man's head and placed it on his own then began eerily stroking Baines' face. 'I think I'd like to keep this one Dad, I don't know though, maybe it's the uniform…'

'You twisted evil bastard!'

'Steady lad.' Arthur said as he pressed it to Matt's brow, it felt cold hard and painful.

Luke stood up and faced Matt, mere inches from him. 'You loved me didn't you?' Taunting eyes wide and challenging.

Arthur just held Matts arms back, letting his son display his madness.

'Are you on something or what? I fell for someone I thought you were, I was wrong, you're a nut case.' Matt figured he was going to die anyway, there was no way that they were going to get their hands on the riches now. 'Your plan just doesn't add up, I've figured out most of it, pretty elaborate, I must say.'

Matt was pushed to the floor. 'Don't it confuse the hell out of you that your friend and boss could fool you?' Luke asked, Arthur checked the curtains seeing the first signs of dawn lighting the sky.

Matt laughed, 'You want me to believe that you,' pointing at Arthur, 'was being blackmailed by the Dingles, because they had found out about how much you were worth? So you faked your own death, set up looney tunes here to woo me to get the money back into the family and then I would have no doubt met an unseemly death.'

'Sort of, yes…' Arthur murmured. Luke just looked from one to the other, then began to drag the policemen's body into the kitchen.

'What are you doing with the body?' Matt suddenly demanded.

'Oh he's not dead, he will sleep for a while, what do you take us for, barbarians?

'Where are you taking him?' Matt repeated although he did feel some relief knowing the Policeman was still alive.

Luke was enjoying this, 'My love is jealous,' he theatrically declared. 'Who knows Matt, when this is over I may have you stuffed and kept as a memento.'

'Tell me, was it really you at the beginning, or did I really meet Jared.'

There was the briefest of glances that Luke made in Arthur's direction before he replied. 'You should have made a wish at the well my love, I take it that you have been back to the old witches cottage?

'Shut up Luke!' Arthur warned.

'What do you mean?' Matt pressed on.

'Oh nothing my love, make a wish and I'll turn into your heart's desire.'

Luke was certainly living in cloud cuckoo land, Matt thought. 'Make a wish and you'd turn out to be a frog!'

'Enough of this,' Arthur demanded 'Luke, get that uniform on, I'll take care of loose ends.' From his pocket, Arthur produced a silencer that screwed onto the barrel of his gun.

'Blimey, just like the Bond films,' Matt said

'Except, this is no movie Mr, Mr...'

'Powers,' came the voice of Luke in the kitchen.

'Interesting, that is.' Matt said with a smile.

'What?'

'You had forgotten my name yes?'

'It's been a particularly long day.'

'Maybe, but do you know what I think?'

'I don't care what you think...'

Luke appeared in the doorway from the kitchen, now in full police uniform. 'It fits a treat Dad, I've even taken his underwear, he's quite a boy.'

'Shut it, I've had enough of your fag frigging behaviour for now.'

'And there we have it,' Matt stated triumphantly.

'Oh God, he's off again' Arthur said, clicking back the safety catch on his gun.

'I don't know how but I've filled in some more facts.'

'Oh deep joy, pray tell, then you die.' Arthur said.

'You're not Arthur Jay are you? I should have realised in a family so abundant with twins, Arthur had a brother.'

'Nonsense boy, you're just wishing...'

'No, Arthur loved me like a son, he even wished I would one day be part of his family,' he looked at Luke. 'And there was a Jared wasn't there?'

Luke looked to Arthur for guidance.

'You are deluded, it's me, I am Arthur Allmes.'

'Ah, I don't think so, he didn't want to be associated with that name any longer. Oh he was pleased for his children to continue the family name in the future but for him, it brought nothing but pain, so he took his wife's name, quite forward thinking in a way.' Matt was on a roll.

'You're blabbering nonsense.' Arthur snapped, stepping forward and raising the gun.

Matt had to think fast, 'His boys were everything, he certainly loved Jared and knew the Will would one day reward him the way he wanted, that's where I came in. He was quite the matchmaker. He also knew that I would seek out other family members and make sure they were taken care of; he knew I would overcome the obstacles that made me unable to gift the rightful amounts to the family, because he loved his family despite everything.

Sirens could be heard in the distance, the police were on their way. Arthur looked from side to side before steadying the gun in his hand.

Matt continued, more for Luke's benefit. 'He loved you Luke, with all his heart,'

'He never showed it.' Luke said

'Be quiet boy!' Arthur shouted and brought the gun to aim and pressed the trigger.

The silencer did the trick, it was quick and silent, the only thing that went wrong was the fact that Luke decided to jump in front of Matt at the crucial moment, taking a fatal bullet in the chest. The police were outside now so Arthur ran out the back way.

Luke looked up into Matt's eyes, blood oozed from a hole in his chest, his lungs were steadily filling. 'I'm sorry,' he finally managed to say.

'Was I right? Did you kill Jared?'

'You're so beautiful, I really liked you,' he began to cough. Was this confirmation that Jared was never here.

Tears welled up in Matt's eyes, more for the fact that another life had been taken, this time, before his eyes.

Luke hadn't quite slipped away, he smiled up at Matt before saying, 'Go make a wish Matt, loo…' Then he died.

9 ISABEL PADLEY

The police had stormed the cottages; Matt could not take in the amount of people rushing around. The only thing that brought him out of shock was a dazed and naked PC Baines being led out with another policeman and a fast acting paramedic who quickly wrapped a blanket around his privates as they made their way to a parked ambulance out in the early morning sunshine. Two more policemen and another Paramedic came up to Matt while two more paramedics checked over the prone body of Luke. The men in front of him spoke but it was like they were so far away, Matt was lost in thought. A dying man had told him to go make a wish, what did he mean?

Two familiar faces swam like moonlight on a reflected pond before him, Barry and Beryl knelt down, worried.

'Hi guys, did anyone ever tell you it was dead quiet in the country? Well they were right about the dead part!' Matt said

An hour later, they were sat at the police station. PC Baines had agreed to radio in, intermittently so when the calls didn't come, Hepton had sent the entire force down to Horton Stoney, fearing the worst. In a comfortable room within the Police station and sat on three sofas, Matt sipped fruit juice while Barry, Beryl, DCI Hepton and Sergeant Blake made themselves comfortable around him.

'No sign of Arthur Jay sir,' Blake said, addressing Hepton.

'Certainly a slippery snake, so do we think this man isn't Arthur Allmes-Jay?'

'It's my opinion that he may be another twin, certain things he did and said were not like the man I know.' Matt sounded almost defensive of his old boss. 'I would hold off on the body being dug out again…'

'Oh you do, do you?' Hepton challenged, with that warning glare shadowing his eyes.

Everyone in the room tensed, except surprisingly Matt, who after the night he had just had, remained sitting and nibbled the chocolate off around an orange flavoured penguin biscuit.

Hepton watched him and then, breaking unwritten laws of physics, began to chuckle. 'You may have a point Matt,' he turned to Beryl, 'Tinkerbell, what do you have for me?'

'Isabel Padley sir, she was a friend of Arthur Jay's mother Dora, up until she had a baby on the very same day, then nothing.'

Hepton frowned. 'What do you mean nothing?'

'Just that, her family trail just vanished, like the Padley's never existed.'

'You could be on to something. When Embridge gave me a run down on Arthur's life he did mention Isabel, I just knew it was something not to ignore.' Matt had been trying to remember her name.

'George, get Embridge, Embridge and even bleeding Jones in here for a little chat will you?' Hepton spoke to his sergeant, who promptly got up and left. 'These Solicitors are tricky buggers, rest assured, if they are sitting on answers, we'll find it. Barry, what have you got?'

'DNA Markers insist that the man buried is Arthur Jay.' He glanced to Matt. 'Sorry Matt.'

Matt gave him a wave of his hand, 'I'm just glad that that psycho on the run out there isn't my old friend.

Hepton turned to Matt. 'You may or may not find comfort in the fact that there is indeed a Jared Allmes, he was meant to be on leave only, he has vanished. The man that died in your cottage is Luke Allmes.'

Matt just looked down, what did that mean to him?

'I pulled up a file on Luke Allmes sir.' Beryl said. 'He has been quite busy with the police in these parts over the years but for a long time simply vanished; it appears that he had in fact been sectioned, twice under the Mental Health Act for violence and inappropriate behaviour.'

'Why am I not surprised?' Matt mumbled, still haunted by the pitiful man's dying words. 'Listen folks, do you mind if I go back to my house, I know police are still all over the place, it's just, well I really need to get my head down.'

'You're welcome to take a bed in one of our…' Hepton gestured down stairs where a row of nice new prison cells sat but Matt declined.

'No ta Chief, I think I just need time out.' Matt wandered out, Barry went to stop him but Beryl held him back.

'Let him go Barry.'

'He's dying inside though, you know that don't you? Barry demanded of her.

'Tinkerbell's right son, let him be, he knows he has friends and he'll come to you when he needs to. Our units are all over the place down there, he'll be fine.

Matt was in luck, a squad car took him home, back to the cottage. Men and women in uniforms were everywhere he looked, once he stepped out the car. Looking over the road he spotted old Wilf and headed straight for the old man.

'I see you've made an impression on our quiet neighbourhood then lad.' He said on Matt's approach.

'Yes, well I'm sorry about that.' Matt looked ashamed.

'Don't let it bother you son, someone threatens one in Horton Stoney, they threaten all of us.'

'Did you know of Luke Allmes Wilf? Matt ventured.

'Aye, that I do, evil little devil he was, got accused of rape, few years back, think it was all show though, he was one of your lot really, I'm sure of it.'

'Now why would you say that?' Matt asked surprised.

'It was a rumour that he was playing in the hay with one of the farmers boys up in Shapwick, never listen to gossip but I'm tellin ya, something didn't add up.'

'And what of Jared Allmes?' Matt still hoped that his encounter with Jared was still Jared and not Luke. There again, the night that Luke beat him up and attempted to sexually abuse him, there was still something between them, something that he found attractive, even amongst all that violence. If the two did exist to him, then both Jared and Luke were definitely identical in every way, except personality.

Wilf studied the look on his face. 'The perfect gent lad, but you know that, you fell for him.'

Matt smiled at the thought of falling for a man. 'Did I Wilf? Did I really or was it all smoke and mirrors on Luke's behalf?'

Wilf tapped Matt's chest with his hand, 'Here is where the truth is my boy, you young'uns sure as hell get things ass about tit, you end up confusing yourselves.'

Matt thought about what he had just said. He really did believe that Jared had been here, it couldn't have been Luke because one thing was sure, Luke was unable to maintain a reasonable impression of his brother, his social skills were corrupted, not that he'd need any from now on.

'Wilf, what can you tell me of Isabel Padley.'

'You picked a rum one there.'

'So you remember her then?'

'Oh yes, a right bleeding madam she was, just because her husband was a Doctor at the hospital. There was a rumour one time that he was having an affair with someone from here, everyone thought it to be Dora Jay but no, they were neighbours.'

'What, they lived next door?'

'Too right lad, where the Allmes boy lives now, she was a bit neurotic if you ask me, flighty too. Funny thing was, they were both pregnant at the same time, people thought that odd, but her husband backed it up, saying it was true and he should have known…right? Doris will know more, you know Doris?

Matt looked blank,

'Doris from opposite your cottage,'

'Oh I see, why would she know any more than us?'

Doris is her sister…

'Good grief, really?

Doris Broadway scuffled over to the gas hob of her small old fashioned cottage kitchen. Wilf and Matt sat as she prepared three cups of milky coffee.

'You'll have sugar boys won't you? Won't be tied with this healthy living nonsense, none done me too much harm and I'm ninety three.'

'And you look marvellous on it too Mrs Broadway.'

'Now don't you be given me your nonsense either, I knows you're one of those batty boys.'

Matt coughed. 'Where ever did you hear that term?'

'I got a telly aint I, we're not backward here Matthew Powers. I seen it on one of them there documentary's, strange reporter though, I'm thinking his name be Alison G, girls name Alison, always was and always should be.' She brought the coffee to the table and sat with them.

'You mean Ali G, but that's not a…'

'Don't rightly care what he shortens it too, had a speech impudent too.'

'Impediment?' Matt suggested.

'Aye, that too, anyway hark at me muttering on, you're here to ask about my sister, God rest her soul, aint you?'

'Yes but how, oh I see, so even gossip from the police station travels fast eh?'

'Gossip? I don't hold with the likes of that do I Wilf?'

Wilf put a hand on Matt's arm to stop him saying anything. 'I think what young'un was trying to say is that he's heard rumours and thought it best to come see you, to ignore all the different tales that people, not as respectable as you may like to gabble on about.'

'Oh Wilf, you're right there. Well I think the first thing to say is Isabel was a naïve, foolish woman.

Isabel was a good twenty years older than me, by the time I had grown enough, she was already married to Doctor Edward Padley, aye he was a right snooty so and so, let me tell you. I know that she and Dora Jay were pretty close while they were both pregnant, people talked, saying that Dora was having a fling with Doctor Padley but nothing was further from the truth, truth is, they barely had time for each other. Kind of ironic then that he was the one that delivered her babies, then went right next door and delivered his wife's.'

Matt instantly swooped on the crux of Doris's story. 'You said babies.'

Doris turned to Wilf with a smile, 'Chose him well Wilf, didn't he.'

'That he did Lass.'

Doris spoke quietly suddenly, as though the walls themselves had ears. 'Isabel was a sickly woman, there was no way she could bear a child, we don't even think she was pregnant. Dora was having twins and, well I don't exactly know the true circumstances and to be honest, I don't think we ever will. Whether Dora was in on the agreement, her daughters didn't seem to know that they had two brothers; they resented one boy so two would have tipped poor Dora over the edge. Poor woman never really got over the death of her husband; she relied on her friend and neighbour and probably agreed to anything suggested to her. Unfortunately, the very next day they were gone,

Doctor Padley, Isabelle and son, gone. I never heard from her until near the end, they had been living on Jersey and the letter sent, informed me that her husband had died five years previous and she was now on her sick bed.'

Matt cut in. 'When was this?'

'Oh, years ago boy, I had auburn hair when Isabelle finally died, alone.'

'And the son, what became of Arthur's brother?'

'Well we don't know, as I say it's only assuming that the twin was given away, there was no grave for a child. I'm thinking that Doctor Padley fixed it. I never told Arthur when he was alive because it was none of me business, only Wilf.'

'Very commendable Mrs B, the only problem is that this definitely is Arthur's long lost twin and he is, what we might call, a homicidal maniac and he's loose, out there somewhere.'

'Oh, my giblets, is it really? You damn near taken all me puff away.'

'I am sorry about that. Look, I've taken up enough of your time, thank you for the coffee.'

Wilf stayed put as Matt walked to the back door, Doris shuffled behind him to see him out. 'Now you find that boy and tell him you love him, Arthur always knew you'd be right for each other.'

Matt looked back. 'Jared has probably been a victim of this nutcase, I'm afraid.'

'There has been enough killing, I sense for you, a new beginning. You go find him my boy, he's waiting, hoping. She said as she finally shut the door.

Matt turned and walked to his house, half smiling and shaking his head, the woman is a witch. His thoughts once again turned to Luke's dying words,

Go make a wish Matt, he had said, wish for what? And then he thought of the well up at the Allmes cottage.

10 THE WIMBORNE DETECTIVE AGENCY

The VW camper van shot up the lanes, leading to the old Allmes cottage. The police back at the Hamlet where he lived did watch as he jumped in his vehicle giving a cursory shout of where he was heading before driving off, through his back mirror, he could see one Policewoman on a radio, which was good; he had no time to explain and was banking on them coming along.

The cottage looked dark and foreboding, even though, by now it was late morning, clouds had once again thickened, but no rain had as yet fallen. He pulled into the wide messy drive. No sign of police then, Matt thought, wishing he had waited for… now what was the police term? Back up, that was it. He got out the van and ran up the side of the cottage to the rear garden, where Perrins wood looked like an ominous spectre overlooking the cottage and land. The well looked innocent, sat at the top of the garden. It was basically a hole in the ground where a ring of white stone had been built up to resemble the traditional wishing wells but without the wooden roof. As he approached he noticed the piece of wood that covered the hole was slightly to one side and to the edge of it was the slightest trace of blood. Matt checked for rope, then thinking light would be good too, blast, he never did keep a torch in his van. He decided to try the cottage and was surprised when trying the back door, it actually opened. Creeping in its gloomy rooms, he found himself in the main hallway where the doilies atop the side board were neatly holding back the hard surface of crude ornaments from scratching the highly polished veneer of the wooden furniture. Matt remembered meeting Miss Allmes here, quite some time ago, and the way she had placed the doily on her head, making out she was in mourning, truth was, he was probably talking to Adeline and not Leticia Allmes, no doubt there was some subtle differences in their appearances that she endeavoured to cover up when he originally called, how was she to know that, apart from the odd silhouette of the woman walking off in the distance or the rumpus at the front of a queue in a shop that Leticia was usually the cause of, he had never really, really looked at her, so the doily was probably not necessary. I wonder which Allmes sister was dead here and what had happened to the other. He pondered. He opened one of the cupboard doors in the sideboard and was pleased to see a large battery operated lamp. Pulling the switch, he was rewarded with a bright wide beam of light. 'Perfect, now for something like rope.' Matt said marching back to the kitchen.

The drawers, broom cupboard and cabinets in the kitchen drew a blank, at that point he thought of the old lean to shed near the coal bunker just outside. As soon as he opened the shed he could see old fishing net hung up the wall, metres of it. He quickly rolled it up and within moments was racing down the garden, afraid but driven, to see if anyone was down the well.

The thick netting hooked easily around a nearby tree stump, no doubt, the same one that Arthur had used all that time ago, then he pushed the cover board to one side, leaning against the small wall he shone the lamp downward into the dank damp gloom. He was disappointed to see that the bottom of the well was dry and more importantly, empty. 'May as well have a butchers,' He said to himself, and then promptly unfurled the netting down deep into the well. The net hit the bottom of the well with a strange hollow thud and soon Matt was over the side and climbing down with ease, easier than a plain rope anyway. The lamp was held with ease with one hand, even though the light danced across the well walls. As he got near the bottom, he noticed the ground wasn't even, he then noticed gaps around the outside of the ground, it was a piece of wood cut to the shape of the floor. Oh no, he had an inkling what it could be concealing. Finding a slight ledge in the wall of the well, he placed the lamp securely then his fingers reached down to the wood edge, it was plywood with loose dirt spread across it. Slowly, he lifted it, a smell wafted up and a sunken face of an aged woman stared up with blank eyes. 'Leticia Allmes.' He said through screwed up face. As the board was finally propped up against the wall he saw a huddled form of another body, it was face down, but the dark tight locks were obviously belonging to the one person he dreaded to see, but at the same time wanted to find. These people would get a respectable send off, the sisters didn't deserve it, but the man he had loved, the only man he had loved, all be it for a day, would be able to rest in peace. He grabbed the lamp from its ledge and stepped onto the proper well floor. His legs felt shaky but he stepped past the rotting Miss Allmes and knelt by the body of Jared. He gently pulled at the shoulder, frightened that Jared would snap. The body rolled over easily and Matt flinched as he could see that Jared had been messed up pretty badly, whether from being thrown down the well or prior to. The way the body had been positioned though, he figured it was brought down. The face had been punched; blood was dried across his once firm brow. Matt wiped some dirt from his face and began to cry. He sat crossed legged placing Jared's limp head on his lap continuing his sobbing, even rocking back and forth in despair.

Just then one of Jared's swollen blood encrusted eyes opened, and his husky barely audible voice said. 'What bloody kept you?'

Police cars descended on the cottage and soon they detected the fishing net down the well. Ambulances were called along with rescue services. Matt didn't leave Jared's side until he was lifted out of the well. The Police were keen to speak to Jared but he was still in a pretty bad way.

Hepton arrived as Jared was being placed into an ambulance, Matt made to follow.

'No you don't Powers, I need you to answer some questions.'

Matt took his foot off the ambulance steps. 'Back to surname calling, I guess I'm in your bad books again.'

Hepton stepped up to him and shoved a pointing figure at him. 'Listen you bloody idiot, I can't protect people that go off on their own mercy missions without police protection...' Hepton was angry because he considered what Matt had done was dangerous, he cared.

'I'm sorry, it was impulsive, I did let you know, I just...' he eyed the ambulance, no longer finding the words.

Hepton, knew why, deep down, he was also glad that Jared was alive, at the moment anyway. 'Has Allmes said anything?'

'Not much, he did say that Edwin Padley, that's Arthur's twin brother was the main killer, he's the one that left Jared for dead, down the well, he had a hold over Luke, I guess he just yearned for a father to love him.'

'Should be easier now we have a name, that particular father figure is out there somewhere. Not in that Ford Escort though, it was found burnt out on Archers Field, I need to double the effort. You go with him then Matt; I'll know where to find you.' Hepton walked off and started bawling at some poor uniformed officers.

Matt smiled and was just about to get into the ambulance when something reflected from the long grasses high up near Perrins Wood. Of course, Edwin was watching them from up in the one place he had used to spy on the cottage. He stepped up onto the ambulance asked the paramedic for a quiet moment with Jared. He lay still, looking more at ease than before. Matt reached over and softly kissed his forehead before whispering, 'I'm going to catch him Jared, and then, I'm going to kill him.' He then stepped from the ambulance and sneaked back to his campervan. He noted that the ambulance was on its way by the time he had backed out and followed the single lane up to the woods. Edwin would most probably be armed and yet here he was on one of those one man mercy missions that Hepton was so angrily passionate against.

The VW Campervan was a well-tuned vehicle and purred and putted quietly into the stony car park. Four cars were already parked there, a small red van was at the far end, where a man and a woman sat talking, a small white funny looking Citroen car was parked near the entrance and was empty, and then a familiar black Mercedes, also empty, was sat where Matt aimed to park. He considered that they could have easily taken Jared's car anytime since Luke took his place; he just cursed himself for not noticing its absence earlier. The red van couple were eating and chatting and had no interest in what he was up to as he stepped out the van. He shot off into the wood in the direction that the observer had been hiding. Matt had put on a baggy sports jacket that had been hanging from his passenger seat, it made it easy to hide the lump of metal that was the tyre jack, heavy enough to act as a club.

As he filtered as quietly as possible through the trees, half his brain was telling him that Edwin had a gun and could just shoot him where he stood, he eventually reached the high brush and gorse that led to overlook the cottage, now for the dangerous bit.

Hepton had a call from Beryl who was in attendance at the hospital. He stepped out of the cottage putting a finger in his other ear due to chatter in all directions as officers were once again searching the entire land around the building.

'What's the latest Tinkerbell and cut the crap.'

Beryl stood by a side entrance at Poole Hospital, she smiled, she understood Hepton's manner now, he had even got a little softer since he sat and talked to Matt yesterday morning.

'Come on, it's not like a woman to take her time before talking, God knows it's hard to shut women up…' Hepton began but Beryl cut in.'

'Shut up and listen will you! News was good, Jared Allmes is likely to make a full and healthy recovery, he has intimated to me that he can fill in some points for us but needed to inform you, Matt is going after Edwin sir.'

Hepton had up to that point been holding back a laugh, the way his officer had just admonished him was nothing short of insubordination but truth was, his work was done, Beryl had finally grown her back bone. Then his face dropped at what Beryl had said, 'But he went to the hospital with Allmes, didn't he?'

'Apparently not sir, one of the Paramedics said he saw him driving up the lane to the woods, if that helps.'

'Ok Beryl, standby and get that love sick moron of a colleague to work on any info that Allmes comes out with.'

'Do you mean PC Berry?'

'Of course I mean him, what are you…' she cut the phone off

'Whoops, bad line' she said to herself as she went back into the building. PC Barry Berry was already on hand, worried that Matt had been the next victim, so she would convey Hepton's wishes when she returned.

Hepton looked up to the woods; 'Get me some officer's now.' men began to form in lines in front of him. 'I need a unit of officers to take to the field leading up to the woods, I'll take a group up the lane in the van, the remainder, I want to form a police block here. Barrett, Barrett, where the bloody hell are you?'

A plain closed man with round spectacles appeared in the crowd.

'Yes sir, I'm here.'

'I am right in thinking that this is the only lane up to Perrins Wood?'

'Yes sir, there are some bridleways though.'

'That's not a problem, get onto the station, I want all those pathways policed, we want the armed units doing it, this man is dangerous, be careful though gentlemen, Matthew Powers our resident Private Detective, in his infinite wisdom has gone ahead once again.'

Hepton finished by giving the description of Edwin to everyone, many of them knew Arthur so was somewhat surprised to learn that it was his twin brother.

Edwin Padley watched in fascination as all the groups of police gathered together, it was a pity that he couldn't hear what they were saying. In his mind he was hoping that it would blow over, he could swoop through and exact his revenge. He cursed himself for not dealing with Matt when he saw him climb into the well, he thought it rather rewarding that Matt would find his boyfriend dead, yes he did the right thing, but then the bodies were brought up out of the ground and Powers didn't look that distraught. He had a pair of reasonable binoculars with him to watch proceedings, stolon from Leticia Allmes, of course. He thought back to where it all began.

His parents Edward and Isabelle were not good parents, his mother was constantly drugged up thanks to a father that kept her sedated, and his father would constantly beat him, along with the mental torture, telling him he wasn't wanted, that the blood in his veins was poison, he then told him of the mother that didn't want him but he wasn't to worry because he had taken care of it. Edwin was quite young at this stage and didn't fully understand, all he did know was that Doctor Edward Padley was a cruel sadistic man, and that he got away with anything and everything in their little private residence on the isle of Jersey.

Many years later, when Edwin was a young man, the years of physical and mental torture had turned him into a cruel quick tempered person, unbeknown to him; he was emulating the very nature of his older twin sisters. He left the Island finally getting work on the trains. It was while working on the trains that the Allmes sisters tracked him down, they had always known of the twin brother and had chosen never to acknowledge the fact to anyone, even playing dumb to their mother, knowing one day they would have fun exploiting the fact. That day had come, a lot of money was at hand and they had recruited the deliciously unstable nephew Luke, son of Arthur as well. The plan had been to take Arthur prisoner and replace with Edwin so as to rewrite the Will. Unfortunately the Dingle woman at her post office had snooped some private posts concerning the fortune; one particular post traced Edwin to the Allmes. This made the plan awkward, who else knew about the illegal adoption of Edwin to the Padley's. Luke panicked and killed Arthur at the cottage, Leticia went crazy so he slit her throat, all the while, the theatrical but cold Adeline looked on, with a smile. Luke then took the body of the cottage owner, and threw it down the well. Edwin eventually sneaked onto the scene, hiding out at the cottage with Luke who insisted on calling him Dad. Adeline and her black poodle then took up residence with her taking on the guise of Leticia, despite the fact that Adeline had a distinctive broken twisted nose, that settled perfectly on her twisted cruel face.

Edwin remembered hiding with Luke when the Powers boy came calling and was somewhat taken aback to find that he and his nephew Jared had eventually developed a carnal relationship, yuk he thought. It was then he found out that Luke was the same way, or worse, while they were hiding in a high-street lane, Luke had tried it on with him, his own uncle, the boy was pretty twisted. One day he would deal with all the family members and help himself to what he deserved, from a family that had abandoned him. It was while he was in the bosom of his real family that he had found out that his adopted dad had visited the area and ran Dora Jay, his true mother down, in his car. It was his twin sisters that had arranged it, although the thought pleased him, he hated the fact that his real siblings had planned it themselves, he hated them, despised the fact that they had a life that was his, denied to him by his elders. They had known and not rescued him, yes they would pay. Luke had dealt with one so it was only fair that he should deal with the other, then that blasted Post office woman Della Dingles contacted the cottage, saying she knew what the Allmes family was up to. By this time he had Luke on a tight rein and so sent him to secretly woo her, find out what exactly she knew then, well, he had taken care of her. At the same time his brother Jared was snooping around so Edwin himself took care of him not far from where he was now spying, the branch he hit him with was then secreted at the murder scene of the Dingles woman.

Edwin stopped his meandering thoughts when birds took to flight, not far from him. Nobody seemed to be around, he checked the cottage again through his binoculars, there only appeared to be four police in the garden he noted. Just then a blur on the lens made him refocus. There were police climbing the hillock to the woods, loads of them, he flung round and took flight. Along the worn grass land path he came to some high bracken and was somewhat taken aback as Matt Powers came out from behind it.

'Well, well, well, if it isn't the bender detective, how's that broken heart hanging together Matthew?'

'My heart is fine you spineless cretin.' He stood poised for Edwin to produce his gun, but the man looked confused.

'So the fact that your lover was found dead at the bottom of the well with his decomposing Aunt doesn't affect you? I probably am spineless compared to you. My brother Arthur was right in choosing you to join the family, even if it was because of your disgusting buggering ways. You're as cold as I am.'

'Jared is alive, no thanks to you.'

'What, impossible, I beat him to a pulp, even broke his fingers. Disappointing though, not once did he scream.'

'What did Luke do?'

'Oh he was busy with you, the stupid idiot was meant to gain your trust and stay with you. He got carried away of course.'

'You do a disservice to Arthur, he was a good man.'

'He was a drunk and philanderer.' Edwin dismissed.

'No, just like the rest of us you didn't really know the man, only Jared got to know him out of the family, the only good person out of the brood.'

'It's a pity I wasn't on hand to kill him.'

'Got your lap dog to do it did you? I get it now, let everyone else do the dirty work, coward!'

Edwin pulled a gun from his pocket. 'Oh no Powers, I do the dirty jobs when necessary, one of my sisters was one of mine, broke her neck I did, so easy, and then that snivelling builder Mick Dingles, what a pig, still, he soon got his bacon.'

Matt pulled the clump of metal from his jacket, not really sure what chance he had against a gun. Whatever he was going to do he had to do soon.

'Did you know, I even killed my father, everyone thought it an accident, but no, I took care of him, the bastard.'

'Are you gonna talk me to death or what.' Matt had had enough of Edwin's cruel boasts.

'Quite the comedian at times aren't you, well your sense of humour has come to an end my friend.'

'Yada, yada, yada, and on he goes again, not realising that nobody is listening to him, all because Mummy and Daddy didn't love him.'

'Shut up!'

'You're an old man now; you have lived a long and pitiful life Edwin.'

'So, you even know who I am?' Edwin began a manic chuckle, 'I'm impressed, you'd make a good detective, pity really.' He raised his gun again. 'I tell you what, you give me your best gambit with that there piece of metal and then I'll kill you.'

The madness had taken hold of Edwin by now, he leered at Matt willing him to come and beat him. Matt took his chance, but instead of coming at him he lifted to throw the carjack. With delight Edwin simply raised his gun and shot Matt anyway.

Hepton had reached the car park with his officers en masse. The lovers sat in the red van decided it was time to move on and not before a brief word from a policewoman, they set off looking sheepish. A woman eventually appeared at the end of the car park with her chocolate Labrador walking ahead, holding his own lead; they made their way to the Citroen but as the police went to question her, there was a gun shot that scared the birds in the tree beyond the empty black Mercedes.

'This way, quickly,' Hepton shouted, addressing armed Police, 'We'll take over here.' One of the armed Officers said as a group of police in helmets and body armour ran into the woods.

Matt lay on the ground, blood oozing from his shoulder. Edwin stood over him, 'Whoops, I lied,' he laughed again, 'I was aiming for your heart mind you.' He cackled again then looked around him, they'll be here soon. I saw the police walking up the hill. I'll tell you what...' he threw the gun down and produced a knife.

Matt looked up, powerless and in pain, this was not how it was meant to be.

'I'll make your death the last of my great gifts, Edwin knelt down, eying Matt's neck, 'I'll make it as painless as possible.'

Matt tried to sink away as he felt the stinging of the knife blade, unable to escape the mad man that was drooling above his head. Suddenly there was a crack; a clear red dot appeared on Edwin's forehead as he was thrown back. In that moment blood sprayed across Matt's face. Matt continued to stare up, unable to move as consciousness began to ebb away. At that dream state between reality and blackness, he could make out black figures running past him, echoes of distant voices barking orders as they ran to wherever Edwin was thrown. A face hovered above Matt, the familiar frown of Hepton blurred into view as the DCI crouched down to him, then blackness.

The sun shone over the beautiful Minster of Wimborne, bird song brightened the morning into a cheerful spring day. The narrow lane that ran to one side of Bunty's Butchers was a bustle of activity as two workmen finished off attaching a new sign.

Matthew Powers walked down the lane to the workmen with a tray of tea and hot buttered muffins, which they took gratefully. Matt stood back to eye the new sign, 'The Wimborne Detective Agency – This Way' an arrow pointed up the lane to the smart new front door which sported a swanky new brass plaque with the new business name.

Bunty came out of the office door and shouted. 'Here Matt, your phone is ringing.'

Matt ran and, squeezing past a teasing Bunty, ran up the stairs to the newly decorated and efficient looking office.

'Hello, Wimborne Detective Agency, Matt speaking, can I help?'

'Hello boy, Wilf here, there seems to be a bit of bother at your house, can you get here?'

'Wilf - What's up, what do you mean by bother?'

'Bit of a to-do boy, stop your yammering and get here.' The phone went dead.

Matt huffed, knowing the absolute intolerance of the old country boy by now, but over the weeks of his recovery he had grown fond of all the folk in Horton Stoney who, without exception, had shown nothing but kindness. It was only a shame that he was yet to reacquaint himself with his next door neighbour.

Jared Allmes had recovered enough to give the relevant evidence to satisfy the Police case, but while Matt himself was recovering, Jared was then whisked away to be looked after by his colleagues in the Armed Forces without any chance of Matt getting to see him.

Matt was soon driving his trusty yellow and white VW Campervan into the little hamlet that was his home. Two Police cars were parked near his home leaving what he had come to regard as his parking space free. The van eased into its space and soon he was out and running up his path. The front door of his home swung open and the angry face of DCI Hepton stood. 'What bloody kept you?' he demanded.

'Of all the confounded cheek, this is my house, what are you doing here?'

Hepton dragged him through the door by the scruff of his neck and suddenly he was in a room of people, some were neighbours, some were friends, all smiling.

The cottage had been recently redecorated and all the furniture was modern, all Matt could think was that he hoped the visitors had wiped their feet, this was a new carpet. Hepton soon ushered Matt through the kitchen to the back garden where a bizarre morning barbeque was well underway.

Bunty was working the bacon and eggs on the gas barbecue with Beryl helping. Everyone cheered and clapped.

'How the hell did you get here before me?'

Bunty laughed, that was why you had the phone call, so I could get my arse here with the burgers.

Through the bustle of friends came Darren while Bess appeared with two glasses of bucks fizz. 'Here you are my beauty, Get some of this down your neck, Darren made it from fresh,' Bess said before smothering him with kisses. Darren slapped him on the back.

'I just don't know what to say, why is everyone here?' Matt asked

'They wanted to thank you darling. You helped sort this nasty business out.' Bess said

Matt looked around. Wilf was with Doris who was busy chatting to a police officer. In fact there was an array of uniformed police officers around and amongst a small group of them appeared Barry and his quiet girlfriend Janice. They walked up to him, Barry giving him a big hug while Janice looked on with her usual nervous smile.

'Careful Barry, the people round here might start talking.'

Barry flushed, suddenly embarrassed but he laughed. 'Well you could say that I have had special permission.'

Matt frowned as everyone in front of him looked his way all smiles. 'What do you mean Bazzer?'

Two hands suddenly covered his eyes. 'Guess who?' came the familiar voice.

'Well those hands are softer than old Hepton's.'

The police in the group laughed and cheered, Hepton who had joined the group just waved his hands in the spirit of the party.

Matt slowly turned to see Jared before him. 'Sorry Matt, this was all my idea.'

They stood almost nose to nose. 'I was beginning to think I had dreamt you.'

Jared tilted his head to one side with a teasing expression on his face. 'Shut up and kiss me.'

The crowd cheered and the party lasted throughout the day and most of the night.

The End

ABOUT THE AUTHOR

Simon is a Barber and still works in the area of Hamworthy near Poole. His customers are his lab rats that get the creative juices flowing, so go get a haircut if you dare!

Printed in Great Britain
by Amazon.co.uk, Ltd.,
Marston Gate.